W9-CBA-536

THE MUSEUM OF INTANGIBLE THINGS

AN IMPRINT OF PENGUIN GROUP (USA), LLC

A division of Penguin Young Readers Group
Published by the Penguin Group
Penguin Group (USA) LLC
345 Hudson Street
New York, New York 10014

USA / Canada / UK / Ireland / Australia / New Zealand / India / South Africa / China
Penguin.com
A Penguin Random House Company

The quotation on p. 68 is from Robert Holden, *Shift Happens* (Carlsbad: Hay House, 2011).
The quotation on p. 109 is from Todd Parr, *It's Okay to Be Different*
(New York: Little, Brown, 2001).

Produced by Alloy Entertainment
1700 Broadway
New York, NY 10019

ISBN: 978-1-59514-514-7

Design by Liz Dresner

Printed in the United States of America

1 3 5 7 9 10 8 6 4 2

For my mother, who taught me how to be a friend

Greater love has no man than this: to lay down his life for his friends.

—JOHN 15:13

Lithium really is stardust. It is the third to last element that an exploding star expels before it goes nova. Only hydrogen and helium come after.

—LAUREN E. SIMONUTTI

LOYALTY

I am a freshwater girl. I live on the lake, and in New Jersey, that's rare. The girls on the other side of town have swimming pools, and the girls in the south have the seashore. Other girls are dry, breezy, salty, and bleached. I, on the other hand, am dark, grounded, heavy, and wet. Fed by springs, tangled in soft fernlike seaweed, I am closer to the earth. Saturated to the bone. I know it, and so do the freshwater boys, who prefer the taste of salt.

I come from a long line of downtrodden women who marry alcoholics. All the way back to my Lenni Lenape great-great-great-(lots of greats) grandmother, Scarlet Bird, a red-haired New Jersey Indian who married William Penn.

I know this to be true because of the red highlights in my hair, and because, if you ever see the statue of William Penn in Philadelphia, the one that dictates the height of all the buildings in its perimeter, you will notice, if you look at him from behind, that he and I have the exact same rear end.

Which is pronounced, as rear ends go. And teeters dangerously on the fence between "athletic" and "unacceptable."

My best friend Zoe has a perfect rear end and stick legs, and long, silky black hair. She is obviously not descended from William Penn. There are no dowdy pilgrims in her ancestry. Whereas I am grounded and mired in this place, she's like milkweed fluff that will take off with the first strong breeze. Stronger than fluff, though. She's like a bullet just waiting for someone to pull the trigger.

When we were ten, we took a break from searching for crawfish underneath some rocks at the edge of the lake. We retreated to our fort beneath the branches of the weeping willow, and we made a pact. We wrote it on some bark. And then mashed it into a stew with forsythia flowers, petroleum-streaked sand, seaweed, and a dead fish. And we vowed: never to let each other down.

There is no stronger bond than the one that gets you through childhood.

This is our story.

ENVY

They say the middle class is fast disappearing, and in our town by the lake, it wasn't very well established in the first place. Our hold on it, the middle class, is precarious and slippery, and though it's beautiful in the woods—and though we are only forty-five minutes from Manhattan—a whole lot of us are not going to make it here.

We've heard about the milky-skinned Corinne MacNulty, who, after barely graduating, now pole dances at High Heels, bending over backward for the liquored-up, potbellied friends of her father who used to drive her to cheerleading practice.

Or Michael Garudo, who died in Afghanistan because he had no other options.

Or Jonathan Bruder, who just walked into the lake and drowned because here, when you go off the deep end, there is no one left to rescue you.

If we were at the right place at the right time, Zoe and I

actually could have rescued him. At fifteen, we had dreams of becoming lifeguards. Me because of my love for the lake, and Zoe because she looked good in a red bathing suit. So we signed up for daily two-hour life-saving classes at sunrise, where we learned to drag limp victims through the frigid water by their hair. We had to practice on each other. And we never learned what to do if the victim happened to be bald.

Since then, funding for lifeguard lessons has dried up.

No one is teaching lifeguard camp or writing grants for us or finding us Big Brothers or Big Sisters. No one is donating wings to our school or funding after-school programs for our enrichment. The philanthropists cannot find our public school in the woods. We no longer have gym at Johnson High. Aside from our own efforts with spray paint, we no longer study art. We cannot learn a foreign language, or take advanced math, or study science that's not biology. In fact, if you get above a certain score on the standardized test, you no longer have to stay in school after lunch because they have no funding for anything that isn't strictly remedial.

This leaves us with a lot of free time.

You can tell a lot about a person by the way she spends her free time. Zoe and I spend it eavesdropping, which we do pretty much from the eaves of Sussex Country Day School.

Sussex Country Day sits on the top of a hill in a renovated farmhouse and barn on seven acres of immaculately groomed grass. It has his-and-hers lacrosse fields, a stable filled with shiny-coated horses, and courts for fancy games they don't show on TV, like squash and fencing.

The kids here don't have a lot of free time, and since they have a biological need to rebel even though their lives are absolutely perfect, they do it by taking extra Ritalin or refusing to iron their monogrammed shirts. They do it by wearing black lipstick or raising the hems of their maroon skirts so high that the pleats barely graze the bottom of their dimpled butt cheeks. They have the diseases of the leisure class, like bulimia and attention deficit disorder, and for some reason, with all their fine education, they don't realize that they are the most boring of all clichés.

Zoe and I come here for different reasons.

I am here to learn, and Zoe is here to learn more about Ethan Drysdale. Plus she does a good business here. She is the one who hems the skirts.

Luckily, Ethan Drysdale's afternoon schedule coincides with my interests in learning Spanish and calculus.

"*Hola, estudiantes,*" says the sable-haired Sra. Vasquez. I like her. She's the only one at Sussex Country Day who insists on calling the kids students and herself Señora. The rest of the teachers agree to be addressed by their first names, like servants. Zoe and I can see and hear perfectly from our perch in the attic behind the slats of an air vent.

We found ourselves in the attic one day because Sussex

Country Day offered to donate some barely used microscopes to our biology lab. Ms. Brennan, the only teacher left at Johnson High who cares anymore, asked me and Zoe to help her transport the boxes of pity microscopes back to our school. While we were up there, I could hear the lesson going on underneath us in C-12.

They were learning about Euripides' *Medea* and confidently discussing the feminist implications of the woman-scorned motif. They were basically digesting the stuff that would keep us forever apart. "Us" with our jobs at the phone company and buying chips for the big game on Sunday and "them" with their SoHo lofts and weekend houses in the Hamptons.

I vowed to come back. Even though I knew I'd never leave this town, I was curious about how they get out.

And now Zoe and I come here every day. We wear uniforms that Zoe's clients have loaned us, and we walk into the school like we own the place. This is easier for Zoe than it is for me. I have to fight to tear my eyes away from the rich red Persian rug donated by the Arnejian family and the cluttered trophy case donated by the Smiths. Zoe just walks in snapping her gum and filing her nails. We saunter through the front door and walk past the office, and no one ever asks us for a hall pass, because here, the students really do own the place.

The entrance to the attic is in the Early Education room,

so we have to time it so that the four-year-olds are taking their naps. We slip through the door, climb up onto their plastic play structure, open the hatch, and hop up, sliding the plywood hatch back in place after us. Inevitably one of the little ones stops rubbing his ratty blanket against his nose and looks curiously at us. They are all in love with Zoe, though, and all she has to do is wink at them and hand them a lollipop, and they keep quiet. A few times after nap, we've heard Ella C. talk about the girls who climb into the ceiling, but the teachers just assume she's been dreaming.

We've made the attic our own little hangout, with a fake bear rug on the floor, spare sets of slippers for moving around, and a Flight of the Conchords poster on the ceiling. I've created a desk out of two file cabinets and a plywood CAR WASH sign that the cheerleaders use for their yearly fundraiser. The attic has become my favorite place to be. The aromas of dust, glue, and freshly cut two-by-fours evoke a mixture of nostalgia and possibility.

"Oh my god." Zoe sighs. "I *love* when he sits like that. It's like his thing is so big he needs to stretch out his legs just to be comfortable."

From between the slats we can see Ethan sitting in the back row, practically spread-eagle at his desk with the tops of his shoulders against the seat back. His splayed-out, khaki-clad legs do seem to leave room for the bulges of fabric that may or may not be his "thing." His brown hair, piecey and textured with product, hangs loosely in front of his left eye. He has just enough scruffy facial hair to outline his superior jawline. His insanely thick black eyelashes frame eyes that are copper. There is no other way to describe their color, so whatever box he checks off for his driver's license is wildly inaccurate.

Zoe snaps her gum.

"Shhhh. They're going to find us," I mime, flailing my arms around insistently.

I am the type A half of our operation. At least about getting in trouble. I don't like trouble. At all. Getting caught, at anything, makes me cry. Which is why I began paying attention in school in the first place. To avoid conflict. And now I have all this brainpower and nothing to do with it.

Zoe mimes something back to me just to show me how ridiculous I look and sticks her tongue out. Then she gets back to searching for Ethan's picture in the stack of old yearbooks in the attic and encircling them with Sharpie hearts. She uses her Sharpie to send me a note:

DEAR ANNE FRANK: What are they saying?

Sra. Vasquez has created a fake hotel and is asking in Spanish if random *estudiantes* have reservations.

They're in a hotel, I write back.

The conversation below us turns to Ethan then, who happens to have been raised by a Guatemalan nanny. Sra. Vasquez asks him if he has a reservation, and in perfect

Spanish, he replies, "You know we do, *mi amor.* I have reserved our usual room for three hours."

Sra. Vasquez turns bright red, and the rest of the room knows enough Spanish to start caterwauling and wolf whistling.

WHAT DID HE SAY? asks Zoe with the Sharpie.

Never mind, I write back.

Tell me!

He asked her back to his fake hotel room, I write back.

"Oh my god, he is so hot!" Zoe squeals out loud just as the class is settling down.

I've never seen Zoe lose her cool about a guy the way she has about Ethan. She flirts a lot, though. "Hypersexuality" is part of this thing she has. We hate labels, but the doctors like to call it a thing that rhymes with *hi-molar schmisdorder* or *zanic oppression.*

I'm not totally convinced she's bipolar. I just think she's more alive than the rest of us.

Sometimes she feels itchy, invincible, and irritable. She feels everything at the same time and often uses boys as a distraction to calm her down. They're a way for her to channel her energy.

She knows how to handle boys, even the jocks, because she expects nothing from them. She has taught me that, to hang out with a jock, even the ones mothered by "feminists," you have to expect that no matter what you do with them, they will lie and exaggerate to their friends about it the next day. You have to expect that a kiss on the cheek will become a blow job in the locker room. And because they have to lie about you in the locker room as part of their survival, they can never again acknowledge you or talk to you in the hall.

Which is usually fine by Zoe. She isn't in it for the conversation. She's usually so cool about it all.

With Ethan, it's different. Perhaps because he is just barely out of her reach. Perhaps because he is notorious in his nefarious ways with women. I think she's attracted to the danger of him, which brings us into new territory and makes me nervous that she's reeling toward another "episode." It's never boring being friends with Zoe.

And now she has totally blown our cover. The entire mostly-white-in-spite-of-the-school's-diversity-policy class turns and looks toward the slats of the air vent.

We don't have time to replace the hatch.

Instead, we grab on to the far edge of the rectangular hole in the ceiling, swing down onto the red plastic slide, and speedily slip to the alphabet rug. We're out the preschool's emergency exit, dashing across the playground, and scrambling down the big grass hill toward the woods when Sra. Vasquez, putting two and two together, her fuchsia scarf blowing behind her in the wind, screams, "Girls. Girls! There are scholarships!" Except with her accent it sounds like she's talking about smart lambs. We know about their scholar sheeps. We don't want them. Because. Well. Because screw them, that's why. Screw them and their beach houses and their ski trips and their insulting noblesse oblige.

Zoe and I pant and giggle behind a big rock. But once the adrenaline wears off, reality sinks in.

"Do you think they'll seal it off?" I ask her. "The entrance to the attic?" Something about that space makes me feel safe. The way the dust dances in the sunbeams. The thought of losing it feels like a punch in the stomach.

Zoe's not the athletic type, and she's doubled over trying to catch her breath. When she finally looks at me, her eyes even brighter turquoise than usual, her sparsely freckled cheekbones blushed from the fresh air, she guarantees me: "No one will take that away from you."

I believe her because she's protected me and my stuff since kindergarten when she kicked Gavin Gilmore in the balls for taking the Mexican jumping beans I brought in for show and tell.

OBLIGATION

"No one really uses the *nipple,* Hannah," Zoe says. "You should twist the top off." I had just squeezed a wet slurping gulp of water into my mouth from my Poland Spring bottle and wiped the excess from my chin with the back of my wrist.

I sometimes need to have things pointed out to me.

It's not that I'm slow, or "on the spectrum" or anything like that. It's just that I'm an only child. I don't have older siblings to observe. I'm out here like a lone wolf, just trying to slake my thirst. It bothers me that there are rules about the slaking. One should just slake it. The thirst. I bet in Europe, teenagers don't judge each other by how they drink from their water bottles. I have exalted ideas about Europe, especially Scandinavia, which I imagine as a perfect egalitarian utopia.

"Even in Sweden, that is kind of disgusting," Zoe continues, reading my mind. She is sitting in the chaise lounge next to me wearing a green bikini and enormous bug-like sunglasses that reflect the work she's doing with gray felt and a crochet needle. The sun glints off her belly ring. You can almost hear it say, "*Ting!*"

She has agreed to sell the hot dogs with me today, a freakishly hot ninety-degree Columbus Day, in which mothers have scrapped their plans to go apple picking and have come instead to the beach to bask in the global warming with their offspring. We parked the cart in the lot closest to the sand and have enjoyed a steady stream of business since nine thirty, which is apparently lunchtime for three-year-olds who wake up at five.

"Hannah's Hot Dogs" combines all of my father's favorite ideas: alliteration, meat in casing, the American Dream, and his refusal to pay college tuition for a girl who will "inevitably be knocked up."

He hatched the hot dog scheme five years ago on a trip to Miami Beach, where he met a young bikini-clad entrepreneur studying for her O-Chem exams in between her hot dog transactions. And for reasons I prefer not to think about, he imagined his daughter in the same position—wearing a bikini on the side of the road, selling meat in the shape of a phallus to predatory commuters on the way to the city.

Often, I sit in a chaise lounge in the turnout of Route 15 and wait for the crunching tires in the gravel that alert me to my next customer. It's profitable, the hot dog business. Especially in the Northeast, where you can procure some quality meats with a real snap to them. I've made enough money after two months to pay for a year's tuition at "Harvard on the Hill," the county's community college on Route 46.

It's nice keeping the cart close to home today. People here in the country keep their expectations in check. No one ever asks me for a tofu "Not Dog." Or a grass-fed beef dog. Or worse, a buffalo dog. The closer you get to the city, the more dog divas you encounter. For a while I tried to keep up with the requests. It's not that I don't believe in healthy living. I ordered the "not" dogs and the organic ketchup, until those things festered and grew moldy in the storage area beneath the pan. I realized that my business plan should be pure. It's a hot dog cart. You know what you're getting. Hot dogs. Condiments. Chili on Wednesdays. And maybe a wink from Zoe, if she has the time to attract customers for me. I do spend a little more to get the dogs with no nitrates. I do not want to be a purveyor of poison.

The lake amplifies the sounds of sharp yelping from the children splashing their big, bluish-white bellies in the dark green October waves. A motorboat buzzes directly across the lake, slicing through the bright autumn foliage reflected in the water's black mirror. The driver stands and seems giddy. Just last week he was probably kicking himself for being the last guy on the block to get his boat out of the water before it freezes. And today his sloth paid off. He gets one last ride in the sun.

Behind us, only one grimy, algae-sided boat still rocks back and forth in the community boat slips. It's my father's, *The Hannah New Jersey*, a dedication to me and a play on *Hannah Montana*, which no one ever, ever gets. I know the rest of the boat owners are taking bets on whether he'll get it out before the lake freezes over. Odds are fifty-fifty. He is one lazy SOB, which is what he would say if he were talking about someone else.

The irony is that he should know exactly when the lake will freeze over. He's a weatherman, trying to climb the ranks of the network on nothing more than his good looks. Which is not unheard of. And he's gotten pretty far. But the future of his career is cloudy with a chance of becoming a limo driver, which is what he does on the side to make a little extra.

"I'm actually working on 'Sloth-slash-Laziness' right now," Zoe announces.

I seriously do not get how accurately she can read my mind. I give her a look to that effect, and she says, "What? I saw you looking at your father's boat . . . I'm trying to make the distinction between Sloth-Laziness-Depression and Sadness-slash-Despair."

Zoe's eight-year-old little brother, Noah, has some kind of Aspergery thing. He could read when he was two. He understands Einstein's Theory of Relativity. He's read all of Stephen Hawking's books. He is obsessed with the cosmos and talks about it constantly without ever noticing if you're listening to him. And yet he cannot process anything at all irrational or intangible. Emotions are elusive to him. Dreaming and imagination, foreign.

To help him, and since he loves museums (he's been to the Museum of Natural History/Hayden Planetarium twenty-seven times), Zoe created the Museum of Intangible Things, for which she creates a new installation in her basement every month.

September's project was "Pride." In the corner, Zoe created a puffed-out human chest with papier-mâché and peach tempera paint. A marionette peacock walked back and forth over a gay pride rainbow, while a video montage streamed footage of a mother watching her son graduate from college, a swimmer winning a gold medal, and an actress receiving an Academy Award. She covered the walls with white paper and asked me to write about when I feel proud.

I feel proud when I get As on my report card. I feel proud when I win a race. I feel proud when I help someone who needs help. I feel proud of you when you listen to other people. Etc., etc.

Noah will talk about the installation for a few days, his way of digesting it, before moving on to his constant chatter about the Big Bang, Carl Sagan, string theory, Stephen Hawking, and the universe.

"So Hannah, do you think a peacock really *is* proud or just seems proud because of the feathers?"

"I think he is proud, Noah. He has nothing to be ashamed of, I guess." But then you have to discuss shame and how it is the opposite of pride.

"He seems to like it when you do opposites," I say to Zoe now. She is still working the gray felt into what looks like a tiny dress.

She considers this for a moment and then says, "No, I think he's ready for subtlety."

Zoe explains that "Sloth-Laziness-Depression" will consist of Barbie and Ken in gray felt outfits installed in a shoebox also covered in gray felt. She found an old flowered couch with the foam bulging from the rips of the cushions, and on top of it, she flopped her mannequin dressed in a Snuggie. An old TV/VCR will stream infomercials, and Zoe will scatter potato chips and empty soda cans around the couch, which will also be sprinkled with cat hair.

For the interactive part of the exhibit, she filled the pockets of an old fishing vest with rocks and will ask Noah to try it on. Behind a screen in the corner of the basement, to distinguish between sloth and sadness-slash-despair, Zoe created a beating heart impaled by a kitchen knife.

"Won't that scare him?" I ask.

"Um. Duh. He doesn't understand fear."

"Maybe you should do that next. Fear can be useful."

"Speaking of scary . . ." Zoe tilts her head in the direction of the entrance to the parking lot without even looking up from her felt.

My father, still in his suit even in this heat, is in deep discussion with an ice cream man who is just setting up shop. I see him lean his reddening face into the order window. I hear the word "permit" and some more chatter and then "Beat it!"

"Isn't that Danny's truck?" Zoe asks. In New Jersey all the public school boys' names end in *y*. Danny, Tommy, Timmy, Louey, etc.

Danny Spinelli has bristly black hair that's cut short and already beginning to recede a little in the corners. It's the kind of hair that never gets wet. When he emerges from the lake, water collects on top of his hair in silvery amoeba shapes before shaking off completely. He has deep dark brown eyes, and a tall, bendy Gumby-like body with long fingers that apparently help him control the ball on the basketball court. He is shy. And I am shy. And so we've been desperately avoiding each other since sixth grade when he kissed me suddenly and recklessly on the mouth while we were playing co-ed tackle football on the beach one day.

Because of his shyness, Rebecca Forman, a loud and busty cheerleader with a big nose and bad teeth, saw an opportunity and pounced on him in ninth grade. They've been together ever since. Our innocent kiss in the Garden of Eden, lost. And we are left forever wanting. *I* am left forever wanting. Danny Spinelli is getting his needs met. And yet he does seem to show up every once in a while just to keep me in his clutches. I hear that warbling ice cream truck loop of "Turkey in the Straw" from miles away and my palms start to sweat.

As my father walks toward us across the hot macadam parking lot, I put on my sunglasses and try to sneak a peripheral peek at Danny without his noticing.

"He can see you," Zoe says, without looking up from her knitting.

"No he can't," I start to say, but then shy Danny, blushing in two perfect pink circles on his cheekbones, waves to me, I think.

"Was that a wave?" I ask Zoe, trying to stay calm. "Did he just *wave* at me?"

"I think he did. You should take a pregnancy test."

"Shut UP!" I tell her but when I turn back, the ice cream truck, tattooed with stickers of this summer's latest chemical delights, backs out of the lot with its tail between its legs, its warbling, tinkling music stuttering as it retreats up the hill on Yacht Club Drive.

"Say 'thank you,' " my father announces as he saunters up to us chewing on a toothpick. "That kid was stealing all your business again. I don't like him hanging around."

"Oh god, what did you say to him?" I ask.

"He just drives that truck around to stalk you."

"Really?" I can't help but hope.

"Isn't that what you're doing?" Zoe asks him in her dismissive monotone.

"What? Stalking? She's my daughter," he says.

"Which entitles you to: A, rides to school, B, dinner time, and C, a few hours on the weekend." Zoe counts each thing out, pointing to sequential fingers with her crochet needle.

My father ignores her. "Hannah, you coming tonight?"

My dad is getting a two-year sobriety coin at AA. "Which meeting?"

"Dover."

"Sure." I actually like the meetings in Dover. It's a more urban environment, and the stories are grittier. People hit some very low lows in Dover and share stories of waking up in whorehouses or having their toes shot off by the mafia. It's much better than sitting in the basement of the local bumpkin Methodist church and running into your ex-drunken gym teacher.

"Don't you think she should be doing something more age-appropriate, like, say, homework?" Zoe asks.

"I need you," he says to me.

Finally Zoe takes her glasses off and looks at him. "You know, Doug, that's the thing. You're not supposed to need her. She can need you, but it doesn't go both ways until you start peeing in your pants. Are you peeing in your pants, Doug?"

"Not yet, Zoe dear." He knows she *hates* it when he calls her "dear."

"Stop, you two. Yes, Dad. I'll be there."

"Great, I'll take you to Crapplebee's. Cheers, Zoe dear."

"Nice boat!" Zoe calls to him as he walks back across the parking lot. "I don't trust him," she says to me, which is fine for her, but I have no choice. And at least he's trying.

"At least he's trying," I tell Zoe now. The October sun burns close and concentrated as it scrapes its way down the sky on the opposite side of the lake. I sell one last hot dog to a little boy in a wet suit, flatten out his damp and crumpled three dollars, and then start packing up.

"That's something, I guess," Zoe agrees.

DREAMS

My mom, Elizabeth Morgan, is not trying. She awakes every morning to the *Today Show* and a live shot of the Gowanus Expressway. In her forty-eight years, she's never driven on the Gowanus Expressway. It's as foreign to her as the Goethals Bridge, the Cross Bronx, and the Major Deegan, all of which wind steaming, broken, dirty, and crowded into the hot bowels of New York City. She fears these roads and never has to encounter their fire-breathing hatred of humans. Nevertheless, she awakes every morning to a live shot of the Gowanus. Someone thinks it is important information. It's not, when you live on Beechwood Terrace.

When you live on Beechwood Terrace, what's important are the dates for recycling and making sure not to put out too many wine bottles at once. She thinks two a week is a healthy number for one person, and so she keeps a collection of remainders behind my old water skis in the basement.

Since the divorce, and the midlife, and the realization that this is going to be as good as it gets—a crumbling house on the lake, an average-in-every-way daughter, and a dead-end job at the DMV—she has wrapped herself in a cocoon. She's been cocooning, and I've been trying to coax her out and spread her wings. Because although that's as good as it gets, there is magic in each one of those things. The lake. The daughter. The job. The moments. There can still be magic in the moments.

I try to tell her that. And she keeps getting up. If for no other reason than to watch Dr. Oz. She has a powerful crush on Dr. Oz.

When I get home, she is making chili. It's from her side of the family that I get the William Penn behind, and hers rounds out her pale pink bathrobe as she shuffles back and forth from the spice rack to the stove in her slippers.

"You're up," I say. She usually spends Sundays in bed reading.

"I'm up," she says. The bluish skin beneath her eyes hangs there like two used tea bags. She can't look me in the eye, maybe because she feels so much guilt about how she's been raising me lately.

"You're cooking," I notice, somewhat surprised. We usually fend for ourselves. She nukes a Lean Cuisine, and I make some pasta with dill and smoked salmon like they probably eat in Scandinavia. It has omega-3s.

"I cook for you," she argues.

"You . . ." I start and then decide not to disturb her alternate reality. Let her believe that she cooks for me. How can she possibly believe that, though? She may have cooked for me a few times in 2009. I vaguely recall a roasted chicken. "Um, how was your day?" I ask.

"I finished my book."

"That's good."

"And I decided to make some chili. For your hot dog cart."

"Really?" She's generally against the cart. Because it's my father's idea and because it embarrasses her. She's often embarrassed. That's her ruling emotion. The only reason she hasn't banned me entirely from selling wieners is because she can't afford to send me to college herself. "Thanks. I really appreciate it," I say.

"No problem," she says and then blows on a spoonful of chili before giving it a taste. "Hey, someone at work was talking about his kid taking the SATs. You took those, right?"

So, what is the opposite of a "helicopter parent"? I wonder. A subway parent? A sinking ship parent? A hibernating bear? "I was supposed to take those months ago, Mom."

"But you didn't?"

"What's the point?"

"Well, I have a little socked away . . ."

Right, I think. If she returns half of the stuff she bought at Marshalls that now sits festering in a landfill-sized pile of unopened plastic bags on the side of her bed. The bottom layer has probably already decayed and liquefied. She has some hoarder tendencies.

"That's okay," I say. "I can go to County. They don't ask for SAT scores. What did Dr. Oz have to say today?" I ask her, changing the topic.

"Magnesium," she says, stirring the chili and looking out at the lake. At sunset, patches of glassy obsidian stillness begin to stipple through the unsettled parts, putting the entire body of water to sleep.

"Magnesium?"

"Yes. It's even more important than calcium."

"For what?"

"Bones, muscles, digestion, sleep . . . things."

"Things?"

"Woman things."

"Gross."

"Speaking of gross . . . "

"What?"

"I did that thing you said I should maybe do."

"Sign up for a class? Go to Weight Watchers? Take a long walk? Call your friends? Water aerobics?"

"No, the other thing."

"Senior Singles dot com?"

She nods, blushing.

"Oh my god, that is SO . . . gross!" I spit out, surprising myself, and bowing my head in a fit of giggles.

"You're the one . . ."

"I know. No, I'm happy for you really," I say, catching my breath. "I'm totally happy in an entirely disgusted kind of way. Way to go, Mom!" I say, hugging her soft, squishy beanbag body into mine.

"Thanks."

"What photo did you use?"

"The blue blouse one."

"Fabulous," I tell her, picturing, in spite of myself, some old dude opening the car door for her and pinching her ass. I shudder. But I'm proud of her.

She wasn't always like this. She was, at one time, many years ago, a great mom. Zoe and I played with her a lot when we were little. She pitched for endless rounds of kick ball in the front yard, wove stems and stems into daisy wreaths for our hair, baited our fish hooks, fired our pottery, laced our beads, shrunk our Shrinky Dinks.

She taught Zoe how to sew. She *got* Zoe before anyone else did and knew the sewing would help her focus and stay in the world. She was alive once, my mom. And we wrote books together. *Mother Ship and Barnacle Girl*, she called the series. It was about us and how we conquered the world together, because I was going through a phase where I would never leave her side.

"I'll be in my room," I tell her now, "trying not to think of my new cyber-stepdad."

"Very funny," she says, and she actually grins a little, then she tries unsuccessfully to wipe it off her face.

My room is neat. I like to keep things in order. I have a special way of folding my T-shirts and a special way of putting them in the drawer and a special way of making my bed so that the seam of the bedspread lies perfectly on the edge of the mattress.

The bedspread is gray. The throw pillows are lemon yellow. My dresser is white, and I have a lemony yellow and white area rug outlined in gray. Everything is spare and minimalist. There is no fuzziness or fluffiness. There are no tassels.

My desk is neat too, and I spend a lot of time sitting at it. On the wall to the right of my desk hangs a large whiteboard calendar with color-coded magnets and dry-erase marker notes indicating my to-dos for the month. I like to have it all laid out in front of me and not tucked away in a computer somewhere.

On another whiteboard is the Wiener Meter. It' a three-foot-tall, dry-erase hot dog indicating with brown marker how many I've sold, and how much more I have to sell to pay for two years at County and two more years at a state school somewhere. I have $2,466. I need $5,454 more, assuming I get some good financial aid. I make a profit of

$2.17 per frank, so I need to sell 2,513 more hot dogs. At an average of twelve hot dogs a day, that's 209.42 more days of selling hot dogs one day at a time.

It's good to be goal oriented. I will study accounting. Get a job at the phone company and get an apartment nearby so that I can continue to take care of my parents.

Zoe says it's good to be goal oriented but that I have the wrong goals.

Tucked in a desk drawer that no one knows about is a red folder filled with information about studying abroad in Sweden. On the wall behind me is a black-and-white signed photograph of Astrid Lindgren sticking out her tongue. And my bookshelf is filled with soft, washed-out, well-loved copies of her books. Not just the Pippi ones, although those were my favorites. (I was Pippi Longstocking three years in a row for Halloween, and one year my father dressed as my horse and I pretended to pick him up with one hand.) But the more obscure ones too, like *The Brothers Lionheart,* in which the heroic young brothers die not once, but twice, to experience two different levels of heaven. In their final death, they jump off a cliff together so they're never left apart.

I guess that red folder represents the goal of my true self. If there were no society, no *circumstances*, no *friction*, I would become an author-slash-illustrator of books about egalitarian utopias like Sweden, where girls are more like boys and vice versa. And I'm really not sure my ideas about Sweden are accurate, so I would start with a study abroad to find out.

Abroad is a word that people at Johnson High don't think about, though. At least since they fired all the guidance counselors and put the school secretary in charge of "guidance." She just goes about her normal business, and if someone has a guidance question, she refers them—with a not so kind gesture—to her pile of applications to County College of Morris.

Just for kicks I open up my file cabinet and pull out a yellowing crackly construction-paper volume of *Mother Ship and Barnacle Girl,* which of course I've kept because I'm like that. My mother's face was drawn in profile. Her torso, the figurehead of the ship, and the hull the rest of her body. As Barnacle Girl, I wasn't really a barnacle but a super girl with a mask and tights made shiny by pressing down too hard on a purple crayon.

"Over there, Mother Ship," says Barnacle Girl in a black crayon speech bubble.

"Our destiny awaits," replies Mother Ship as she beaches herself on the shore.

Well, you can't argue with that, I think, and I tuck the book back where it belongs, still wondering how it will all turn out.

DISAPPOINTMENT

I wear my (schm)UGGs because I don't want to make any noise crossing back and forth across the gym. Even though I like the sound of my high heel hitting a floorboard when there's a hollow underneath it (*clonk*), I don't want to call attention to myself today.

I shouldn't have worried about it, though. Only ten of us showed up to "Paloozapalooza," Johnson High's combined Art Show, Science Fair, and ClubExpo run by Ms. Brennan.

The gym is dark. They only bothered to turn on half the lights, and some of the fluorescent tubes are buzzing and flickering as if they have mosquitoes fluttering around inside them.

A ripped and peeling student painting of an eagle making a muscle hangs on the far wall. A lonely red and gray banner hangs over the bleachers. BASKETBALL STATE CHAMPS 1987.

Outside it's windy, but warm. Sandstorm weather even though we're far from a desert. Every once in a while we can hear a gust of wind slap and whistle against the windows, which are high above us. In the hallway above the gym door, Ms. Brennan's eight-year-old scrawled a pink Paloozapalooza poster in bubble letters with the final "ooza" squished together because she didn't leave herself enough room.

Each of the ten Paloozapalooza participants is setting up a card table "booth." In science, I am "presenting" my findings of my study on fruit fly genetics; in art, my *Self-Portrait in the Lincoln Tunnel*; and I am supposed to hand out flyers to recruit people for the school newspaper, which right now I create entirely on my own. So far I've given a flyer to Thalia, Ms. Brennan's eight-year-old. And to Julian, who is here to recruit for the school's first GLBT support group. He is wearing a fedora and a skinny tie to look official. And spreading out a fan of "It Gets Better" brochures that have been graffitied with black Magic Marker cocks in people's mouths and the word *fag* scrawled all over the place.

"How could it possibly get better than this, Hannah?" he asks sarcastically, holding up his fan of tarnished materials.

"I don't know, Julian. We are the lucky ones." I sigh. "Here. Want to join the school newspaper?"

"Sure. Want to join GLBT?"

"Sure," I say.

"Really?"

"I just like the message. It's got to get better, right? How could it possibly get worse?"

"Oh god. Don't say that," he warns, and just then Amanda Le, the school's entire Asian contingent, starts playing "Für Elise" on the bassoon. Hers are the only parents who showed up, and they huddle next to each other, standing in front of their daughter, holding one of Julian's brochures, listening intently to the music.

When Amanda is finished, Julian and I break into applause and whistles, which makes Amanda smile a little and take a little bow next to her bassoon.

"Show me your work," Julian says, so I escort him over to my fruit fly exhibit.

"Some fruit flies have blue eyes and some red. And some of them," I say, turning the page to another graph, "have same-sex partners."

"*This* is groundbreaking," Julian says.

"Not really. They could just prefer the company of men," I start.

"Who wouldn't?" Julian finishes. It's an old Homer joke from *The Simpsons.*

I show him my self-portrait.

"So Freudian," he says. "The tunnel. It's a celebration of the mysteries of the vagina."

"What?" I laugh. "I just like the Lincoln Tunnel."

"Of course you do. Here. Take a brochure," he says, lifting and lowering his eyebrows.

Ms. Brennan has dressed up a little for the event. She's

wearing a peasant top and a straight denim skirt with brown leather boots. She's flushed and innocent and trying to muster up some enthusiasm for us. Even though she spent a week begging the custodian to set up the microphone and speakers, there is now absolutely no need for them.

She has prepared a little speech, so she starts to talk without the microphone as we gather around her. Her husband, the only other adult in the room aside from Amanda's parents, hoists Thalia up onto his shoulders. Mrs. Brennan clears her throat, blushes, and begins to read from a folded piece of printer paper. "Welcome to the . . ." She stops, looks up at us with our heads down, ashamed to be participating in this lame event rather than the packed-to-capacity pep rallies for the football team. "You know what? I'm going to use the effing microphone!" she announces.

She tosses her piece of paper aside, stomps to the microphone, and turns it on. It squeals for a second and then calms down. "And do you know why I'm going to use this fucking microphone?" Amanda Le's parents look at each other with concern. "Because you guys fucking deserve it. You guys . . ." She has to stop and wipe a tear and take a deep breath. "You guys are my fucking heroes."

Ms. Brennan's husband is smiling—giving her some hand signals that seem to mean "ix-nay on the ucking-fay," but he seems proud and amused nevertheless.

"Really. You guys are warriors. Warriors against the cult

of stupidity that is taking over our nation. And I'm proud of you. I don't care if the rest of the school isn't proud, or that your parents don't give a shit. In spite of that, you showed up. And you care. And you should be proud of yourselves, because obviously, no one else is going to do it for you. You guys are strong, intelligent, caring warriors, and I'm *so* happy I got to know you! I'm proud of you, and Mr. and Mrs. Le over there are proud of you." Mr. and Mrs. Le nod enthusiastically. "And Joe and Thalia are proud of what you've accomplished."

"I'm proud, too!" a voice announces behind us. Zoe suddenly sweeps into the gym with Noah, the clonking of her high-heeled boots echoing across the otherwise silent, practically empty, pathetic, half-dark gym.

"And I'm proud as a peacock," Noah says. "I learned *proud* last week!" He walks and then gallops a little, his hand letting go of Zoe's to engage in some enthusiastic flapping. A little chick trying to take flight.

"Sorry we're late," Zoe says. She hugs me. I was hoping maybe my dad would come. I knew Zoe would show up, though. She's very good at feigning interest in my pursuits. She is, when I stop to think about it, my entire family. Some people have whole rooms full of people to feign interest in their pursuits. Large Italian families full of sisters and brothers and cousins and aunts and uncles. I have Zoe. And Noah, of course, but feigning isn't his best talent. He tries for a second to be interested in genetics, but then darts over to Simon O'Malley's exhibit on "String Theory and the Ever-Expanding Universe," which Simon basically copied verbatim from a PBS *Nova* special.

"Here," Zoe says, and she hands me a brown shopping bag with pink ribbon handles from some boutique.

"What's this?" I ask, peeking inside.

"Clothes," Zoe says, without looking away from my painting. "This is so good. The brushstrokes around the eyes and the fluorescent light from the tunnel . . ."

"Thanks," I say. "Why clothes?"

"Party. Eight o'clock."

"What's wrong with what I'm wearing?" As much as I like rules, I have trouble with the rules of fashion. I wear clothes to cover my skin and stay warm. If it's cold, I wear more clothes. If it's warm, I wear less. I'm not particular about the intimate details. Which I'm sure is true of teenagers in Scandinavia. There, it's too cold to be vain.

"Full details or big picture?" Zoe asks.

"Big picture."

"Well, UGGs are for walking home from the beach after surfing in Australia. They are shapeless and bland and sloppy and will give you shin splints if you wear them for more than an hour. We've also talked before about avoiding trends and dressing for the shape of your body. If you're wearing pants, they need to be . . ."

"Boot cut or flare," I finish.

"And those?" she asks, pointing to my legs and taking a sip from her water bottle, which I'm guessing is filled at least partly with vodka.

"Are skinny jeans."

"And you are . . . ?"

"Not skinny."

"Which is . . ."

"Good. I should accentuate, yet balance my curves with proper proportion."

"Right. We need to go."

"Where?"

"Ethan is having a party."

"Ethan Drysdale?"

"Yup."

"What about Noah?"

"He can come. Let's go, Nos," Zoe lifts her poncho-covered arm like a bat wing and gestures for Noah to wrap up his ramblings about the cosmos. I consider her poncho and why that would be an impossible choice for me. Where would I put my backpack? Under it? Like a turtle? Or a soldier trudging through the trenches in the rain?

She does look good, though. Everything she's wearing is the same tone of steely gray. Even her fingernails. Which are polished. Something I've never even bothered to try since they'd just get chipped in ten minutes anyway.

I pack up my stuff and obediently go to the girls' locker room to change for our Ethan Drysdale manhunt. I have my reasons for accompanying her. There's the anthropological curiosity: How do rich kids behave at a party? There's my own romantic fantasy: Maybe Danny Spinelli will be there; he and Ethan used to play Little League baseball together, and they still hang out sometimes. And there's my obligation to Zoe: my talent for keeping her safe and checking her outlandish impulses that began the very day I met her at age seven. I was collecting reeds for a project on papyrus at the marshy, swampy part of the lake at the end of our street, and I found her posing nude for a teenage boy who promised to give her a dollar.

"Hey!" I interrupted him just as he was about to take a photo, and he ran like a deer through the reeds, the susurrations of his retreat rustling around him until he made it to the street.

"That was stupid," I told her as she pulled on her T-shirt.

"I know. I should have gotten the dollar first," she said, and from then on I knew I needed to watch out for her in a different way than she needed to watch out for me.

The girls' locker room is so deeply embedded with live microorganisms squirming in the grout between the gray and yellow tiles, I expect one day it will become sentient, and the walls actually *will* talk. Hopefully they will send a positive message to future students:

Girls in your underpants, I speak to you from the walls.
Listen to me and to those who have come before you . . .
Surrender not your power to popular girls or to boys who cannot help but use you . . .

"Hannah! What's taking so long?"

Zoe interrupts my reverie long enough for me to finally notice the clothes I'd been unthinkingly squeezing myself into. A lacy white push-up bra beneath a crisp, white blouse and a camel-colored merino wool pencil skirt.

"What the heck am I wearing?" I ask.

"We need to stop at the bar."

Zoe sees my breasts as an opportunity. A year ago when I developed them—I could actually feel the tingling of cells wildly dividing and creating more and more mass to push against my bra—Zoe, who will never have breasts (they are just nowhere in her family tree), did not get jealous but instead was struck with an idea.

She squeezed them together with a push-up bra, dressed me in a low-cut business suit, handed me her mom's reading glasses, and drove me to Mickey's, the local dive where my dad used to take me for a lunch of maraschino cherries while I spun around on the bar stools.

I could barely see as I stumbled in wearing the glasses

and asked for a case of Corona. Seventy-year-old Mickey was too distracted by my boobs and too convinced by my professional getup to ask for any ID. He brought the beer right out and loaded it into the car as if businesswomen every day are walking into dive bars asking for cases of beer. So now I'm a regular, even though I never drink. The case of beer I'm able to acquire has gained us entry into any party we want.

"Don't you think these rich kids can get their own beer?" I ask.

"We are more alike than we are unalike," Zoe postulates.

"Since when, Maya Angelou? Since when are we anything like them at all?"

Zoe ignores me and rushes me out, handing me some jeans to change into when I'm done buying beer. Clicking this time across the gym in the heels Zoe has brought for me, I say good-bye and thank you to Ms. Brennan, who is playing some kind of complicated patty-cake game with Thalia. She seems to feel a little better now, about the turnout of the event.

"It was the first one, don't forget," I tell her. "Next year it will have some traction going in. You can build on it."

"That we will, Hannah! Have a nice night!" she calls.

FEAR

In the car, Zoe's old Chevy Nova spotted with primer, Noah tells us his theory of extraterrestrial space travel.

"Guess what, Hannah?" he asks. Zoe has trained him to start this way, a small prompt to at least try to engage in conversation rather than just blurting out his theories without regard for the other person.

"What, Noah?" I ask.

"Did you know that we will probably never see a being from another planet . . . because other solar systems are *so* far away? No one can even really fathom the size of space. One light-year is six trillion miles, and the closest star is four-point-four light-years away. And if beings from another planet *could* get to us, they wouldn't have any *need* to get to us. That's the paradox. If they had the enormous amount of energy resources to travel twenty-five trillion miles, they would not need to exploit our planet for energy because they had already figured that out. And if they figured out the energy problem, it follows they could probably solve the water problem and food problem. There's really no reason for them to look for us."

"What about slavery? Would they need us as slaves? Or pets?"

"We're here," Zoe says as we pull into the sloping bar parking lot right in front of the Dumpster. A requisite rat scurries underneath it.

"Oh. Pets," I hear Noah considering. He's still talking as I climb out of the car.

The wind slams the door shut. It's an ominous wind. The kind that turns over the leaves of the trees, exposing their backsides and threatening a storm. I turn up the collar of Zoe's mom's trench coat and step into the bar, making sure that my cleavage is exposed. I walk into the packaged goods side of the building, where Mickey himself stands at the cash register reading the paper.

The place smells of metal beer kegs and mildew—the yeasty, stale smell of beer, cigarettes, and middle-aged bad breath. The air tastes like a dirty penny. It is decorated with the free promotional neon signs from beer companies and one very large buck's head above the center of the bar, which is directly behind me as I ask for a case of Corona in my raspy, mysterious starlet voice.

"Right away, dear," Mickey says, and I like him because he doesn't bother to strike up conversation. He signals to his slow nephew bar-back to grab the case from the walk-in refrigerator and put it in the car, and I pay him in cash. As I'm paying, though, I can feel myself being watched.

My father's eyes are blue. Not a blank clear aqueous blue, but a flickering and infinitely faceted blue like the fake gems in class rings. His stare penetrates the collar of my trench coat and burns in two icy hot spots on my neck. I know he is there before I turn around.

Seeing him drunk again is my greatest fear. For two years I've been treading lightly around him, tolerating his biting insults, catering to his loneliness and neediness, earning my own money for college with his wacko scheme, just so I wouldn't have to witness what I know is happening right behind me at this very moment.

It's like being dropped into a black hole. A vacuum of existence. When I turn around, I will be instantly orphaned because I'll know no one can hack it. And no one is in charge. But it's worse than being orphaned because at the same time I am tethered to his failure. His problems are tied around my heart. I will never get away. I am afraid. But I turn around.

He holds my gaze for a second. His eyes and pinkening face look swollen. His thick fingers are clumsy as they stir the melting ice in his emptied rocks glass. He opens his mouth to say something to me across the room, but then his eyes burn in anger. He can so easily turn this into my fault. If I hadn't witnessed it, it could easily have been denied and forgotten. But since I am here, I am witness, and he is defeat. He lets his head drop to the bar for dramatic effect.

And I learn that facing your greatest fear is liberating. You no longer have to worry about it, because it has already happened. And you have survived. I want to face some more fears, it feels so freaking liberating. I want to just jump off the freaking Brooklyn Bridge.

I also want to cry. But I have to wait till I get into the car.

"What about breeding?" Noah says as I climb back into the passenger seat. He hadn't stopped talking the entire time I was in the bar, his jaws robotically moving up and down without changing his blank but beautiful facial expression. "What if the extraterrestrials need us to help them reproduce or something, then they could . . ."

"Shut up, Noah," I say, which is seriously against the rules of this vehicle.

Zoe, who'd been busy backing the car out of the driveway, slams on the brakes and looks at me. "No one tells Noah to shut up," she says.

"Just this once, I need a tell-Noah-to-shut-the-hell-up card," I say. I don't lose my composure, but as I stare at her, one tear slides down over the hump of my chubby cheek.

"What happened in there?" Zoe asks.

"Never mind," I say.

From the backseat, Noah starts up again. Something about wormholes and dying stars.

"Shut the fuck up, Noah," Zoe says calmly, and she puts the car back in reverse then peels out of the parking lot.

Noah stays quiet for about three miles and then sheepishly asks, "Do you feel sadness-slash-despair, Hannah?"

"A little, Noah, yeah. I'll get over it, though. Thanks for checking in."

"Hannah, guess what?"

"What, Noah?"

"Black holes . . ."

NEGLIGENCE

Ethan Drysdale's house, like mine, is on the lake.

As a young groom, my father bought a summer cottage at the bottom of a hill and promised to convert it into a real home. That's numero uno rule of real estate, though: Don't buy a house at the bottom of a hill. At the bottom of the hill, at the edge of the lake, our tiny house is constantly slipping in a murky puddle of mud. He used to spend his free time on Saturdays, hungover and sour, channeling the masonry skills of his father, trying to build runoff diverters and tamp the constant flow of water into the basement. But he's given up now. Now that he doesn't have to live there and step over the puddles in the concrete to get to the washing machine.

My mother and I are used to it.

Everything in Ethan Drysdale's house closes properly with a soft and heavy click. Like a quick French kiss.

The French doors. The drawers. The secrets. The Jacuzzi cover. The boathouse. All of them open and close quietly as rich kids set up for the party. The house is nothing less than a compound. There's an ancient stone carriage house. An art studio. A garage. A tennis court. An outdoor kitchen. A heated pool. Everything aglow with an underwatery light. Someone has strategically placed fishbowls on the tables, each filled with one bright blue betta fish.

The boathouse has a deck on top of it from which a waterslide dives and laps at the lake like a bright turquoise dragon tongue. The three boats and two jet skis have been stowed away in dry dock for the winter, but a water trampoline still floats absurdly off the port side of the dock, tonight's wicked wind trying to whip it into the air like a giant black Frisbee.

Couples congregate on the patio in chaise lounges situated close to outdoor heaters shaped like big silver trees. The wool blankets they use to keep themselves warm give them an excuse to let their hands wander into each other's laps.

I don't know who stripped first, but the Jacuzzi is full of glistening naked adolescents sitting shoulder to shoulder with looks of faux bravado on their faces. Some girl is dropping toasted marshmallows into their mouths as she walks around the perimeter in her string bikini and crocheted cover-up. The missed marshmallows melt in the hot water and create a brownish white meringue foam that floats on top of the water.

We do not blend. Me in my crisp white blouse holding a case of beer, Zoe in her poncho and high gray boots that come over her knees like a swashbuckler, and Noah, who has a cold and who sniffles as he wipes away some snot with the back of his hand. We stand on the deck above the pool and look out across the lake, waiting for someone to notice us.

Across the lake *the amusement park rises bold and stark; kids are huddled on the beach in a mist* . . . It's a line from a Bruce Springsteen song that all of us know, whether we admit to it or not. We are from Jersey, after all.

The amusement park is old, crumbling, and abandoned. It kills Ethan Drysdale's parents that they have to look at it every day. The rumor is they're trying to buy it and turn it into condos. Which are much less interesting to look at, I would think, than the ghostly remains of a carnival. It's beautiful to me. The serpentine humps of the old roller coaster. The rusting silver rocket swings still hanging and creaking in this wind. It's a dream. Or a nightmare, depending on your perspective. I want to draw it.

"Were you invited to this soirée?" I ask Zoe.

"Define *invited*," she says.

"*Invited* means: having requested the—" Noah begins.

"Not in the strictest sense of the word," Zoe interrupts. "I was loosely invited."

By whom, I was about to ask, but then I saw him. Tommy Flanagan. He is the link. The crossover. The only one of us who can move fluidly between the schools. The public and the private, because, I surmise, he's the one selling the marijuana, which he shouldn't be selling to some of the dudes here, because I recognize them from their mandatory attendance at my father's AA meetings.

"Ice!" Zoe waves to him, and he gives a little salute, coming up through the basement to meet us on the deck. His hair is prematurely white. People used to call him Salt-n-Peppa when he had begun to go gray in ninth grade, but that was too long, so they abbreviated it to Peppa, and then when he lost all trace of black, he became Ice.

Everyone loves Ice. Except for me. I don't love him the way he loves me. He stops by the hot dog cart once in a while just to make sure I'm all right, and he calls me Mary. For the Mary in "Thunder Road" or "Mary Queen of Arkansas." His Bruce Springsteen–obsessed firefighter uncle died on 9/11 and left him all his albums and memorabilia. And now Ice is a Bruce fanatic. Which is kind of anachronistic. It's as if he just arrived here from a place called 1979.

I've told him it's an insult, calling me Mary. Bruce himself admits she "ain't a beauty," but hey, she's all right.

"You ain't a beauty right *now*, Mary," Ice answers, "but I have a keen vision of the future, and you are going to outshine all of these losers in ten years."

Ice believes in me. Which is nice. I'm flattered. But just because I'll probably be stuck here for eternity doesn't mean

I have to date the townie drug dealer. I think of him as a creepy older brother.

"Mary," Ice says, and he takes my hand and plants a soft kiss on the back of it. I shudder.

"Hi, Tommy," I say.

"Let me take this for you," he says, and he hoists the case of beer on his shoulder and escorts us to the patio down by the pool where Ethan is grilling shish kebabs, trying to marinate them with a brush while holding the lid of the grill open against the wind. This does not happen at townie parties. At townie parties there are cans of beer and people playing drinking games around a Formica kitchen table.

Zoe doesn't waste any time. She glides over to the grill and begins to seduce Ethan with some suggestive wielding of the pepper grinder. I watch her work her magic for a second—Ethan is already licking something off her fingers—and then I search for a room with a TV where I can deposit Noah.

I find a cozy guest room deep in the recesses of the house and tuck Noah under the quilt of an enormous king-sized bed. Lucky for me there is a *Star Trek* marathon on channel 13.

"Here, Noah," I say as I fluff his pillow and turn on *Star Trek*. "If you need me, just call." I write my cell phone number on a piece of paper and tape it to the landline in the guest room and then go in search of some rich-kid libations.

For the first time ever, I'm not afraid of getting drunk. I'm kicking fear's ass tonight. Why should I be the only one holding things together? Why can't I let my hair down, straggly as it is?

Outside, Zoe is in the pool with Ethan, which is bold, but at least they're semi-clothed and in public. Steam rises from the water like a witch's brew. The wind is whipping up ripples all around them, and people are starting to head inside. One of the tall space heaters topples over. Some of the private-school girls, their long hair gleaming and glossy as if polished with wax, giggle and point at the couple now kissing in the pool. I overhear the word *slumming* when Tommy hands me a Coke.

I'm about to run over to Zoe and intervene. Give her the signal that she needs to slow down. We have a signal—an entire language, actually—that we developed to help Zoe check her most outlandish impulses. I'm about to step in, when Tommy says, "Now that's a power couple."

"You think?" I consider, as I watch Zoe wrap her legs around Ethan's torso. They seal their foreheads together as he pushes her through the water toward the steps at the far side of the pool. He seems gentle, and this is obviously consensual. They are immediately intimate, their bodies bent around each other in the shape of a heart. "You really think she's okay with him?" I ask Tommy.

"Ethan?" Tommy asks. "Take a look around. She could do a lot worse."

But just then, Zoe unhooks her bra and throws it into a tree, letting out a wild cackle.

"I'm going in," I say.

"Leave them," Tommy insists. "He's a good guy."

"Okay, but then I'm going to need something stronger than this," I say, holding up the Coke.

"Not for you. I'm protecting your womb and your skin from the ravages of alcohol." He is utterly smarmy. The smarmiest.

"Get me a beer," I tell him, "and one of those Red Bull things."

He looks at me without moving.

"Now."

Just then, an enormous white streak of lightning zippers across the sky like a crack in an eggshell, threatening to cut the dark in half.

"Okay," Tommy says. "You don't have to invoke the power of the heavens."

A wild crack of thunder then spanks the house and echoes across the lake.

Ethan and Zoe finally climb giddily out of the pool, but I lose track of them. I think they've headed toward the boathouse.

"I hope your friend knows what she's getting herself into," one of the private-school girls laughs snidely.

"She can handle herself," I say as I twist open my first

ever beer. Luckily it's cold enough to mask the taste of it. I plop down on a couch in the basement, drink two of them really quickly.

I grab one of the Red Bull concoctions and begin sauntering around the house. No one sees me. It's like I'm moving around behind the wallpaper, in another dimension, but I can see everything that they do. My body feels warm. My limbs get slow and heavy, and there's a numbness in my teeth.

One by one, glossy-haired girls pair off with newly muscled adolescents who pin them against the wall and try to swallow them with open-mouthed kisses.

I stumble my way to the gigantic kitchen, which is made of stone. They even have a fire brick oven for making pizza, and a stone hood built around the stove. "Who lives here?" I ask out loud. "Oprah?" No one answers.

Copper pots and pans glint and gleam in the track lighting as they hang in orderly rows from a wrought-iron ladder above the stone kitchen island. A group of teens engages in the sharp banter of the elite. They stand tall and look each other in the eye. Like teens in Scandinavia, I think foggily. Since preschool, their teachers have been paid to tell them how truly amazing they are, and so they have the supreme confidence of kings and queens.

A broad-shouldered lacrosse-playing specimen leans comfortably against the counter and says, "My dad rents to them. They get all their rent paid through Section Eight, so it's a guaranteed paycheck for him every month."

"What's Section Eight? The government pays part of the rent?" another boy asks.

"The government pays *all* of it," lacrosse boy says, waving his beer in the air. "These women just keep having kids with different fathers so they can live for free off the state."

"That's interesting," someone loudly blurts. *Wait, was that me?* Am I daring to debate lacrosse boy? Everyone looks at me and gets quiet. I put my head down but continue quietly. "So the women are solely to blame?" I ask.

"Yes," he answers.

"And not the men who get them pregnant and refuse to support their children? The *men* are within their rights to walk away and let the kids be supported by the government? I guess they didn't want to have sex. They were tricked into it by these duplicitous women. Interesting," I say and then move toward the steps that lead to the basement. I can feel a whole group of eyes on me. It is silent until someone says, "Was that the hot dog girl?"

I walk downstairs and look out the sliding glass door. The rain pelts it now and slides down the pane in complicated tributaries. I press my forehead against the glass to cool it and watch as more lightning spiders through the sky. A blue crackling vein. A white tree. An orange zipper.

I'm just about to head out and look for Zoe—it's been too long—when someone taps me on the shoulder.

I jump and turn around.

It's Danny Spinelli.

The alcohol has jumbled everything. Turned it upside down. Suddenly everything is hilarious. Ethan. My father. Zoe traipsing braless around the backyard. Rich kids leaning against the counter, their elbows bent up behind them, purposefully flexing their triceps. Hilarious.

"Um," Danny starts, his face blushing again but only in those two cute circles on his cheekbones. "So what's funny?" he asks.

And *that* is funny to me, too. Asking what's funny is *so* outrageously funny because how am I going to explain that *everything* is funny, because if it's not, it's just too, too bone-crushingly sad to tolerate.

"Vitameatavegamin," I slur.

"What?" he says. His eyes wink a little as he sideways grins.

"You know, the *I Love Lucy* episode," I say. "Or do rich kids not watch that? I'm outta my league here," I say, moving my beer bottle around in a sloppy circle to indicate *here.* This party.

"I'm not one of them," Danny says and smiles. "And I know the Vitameatavegamin episode."

"I just thought since I am a little, like, schnockered, I would try to say Vitameatavegamin. Try it," I say. "Vita . . ."

"Vita," he says, looking down.

"Meata."

"You're kooky," he says.

"Kooky? Who says 'kooky'?"

"I do," he says.

"Meata," I say again, touching the lip of my bottle to my own bottom lip.

"Meata," he obeys, peeling some of the label off his beer bottle.

"Good," I say. "Vegamin."

"Vegamin," he says, and when he does, he looks up. He looks me square in the eye for the first time since that kiss in sixth grade. And every cliché thing from the romance books happens at once. Time stops. We're alone in a vacuum-like orb. It's like being inside a snow globe. Things fade in the periphery. My body falls away, except for a slight tingling, you know where. My eyes water. My pupils probably dilate to the size of quarters to let as much of him in as possible. When, dammit, the thunder claps again, and Rebecca's cheerleading voice echoes down the staircase, popping our wondrous love bubble.

"Danny!"

"Crap," he says. "I gotta go," and he rushes up the stairs two at a time. "Call me," he says. I *think* he says, "Call me."

I sit on the couch in complete awe of what just happened. And I'm suddenly extremely heavy with exhaustion. I want to fall asleep as soon as possible. I promise myself I'm just going to close my eyes for five minutes before I go out and find Zoe. I just want five minutes to dream about Danny. Sometimes I can do that. Think about something as I'm falling asleep so it will show up in my dreams.

Instead of dreaming about Danny, though, I have one of those terrible hot-dog-cart stress dreams where there's a line of people snaking around the corner waiting for hot dogs and I can't seem to fish even one hot dog out of the boiling water without something else interrupting me.

When I wake up, my phone is vibrating like crazy in my pocket.

I wipe the saliva off the side of my face and try to remember where I am. I don't recognize the phone number blinking on the phone, begging me to pick up. Something smells eerily familiar. It's only when I sit up and realize I've been completely covered in raw hot dogs, a bunch of them falling to the floor and bouncing off the carpet, that I remember where I am. "Noah!" I scream, and then finally pick up the phone. "I'll be right there, buddy," I say and stumble my way through the house, climbing over sleeping bodies, searching for the room I left him in.

It's not quite the aurora. It's in between the aurora and daybreak. The sky, still a purply gray, is streaked with pink. The storm has blown beer bottles and paper plates and towels and the wool blankets all over the backyard. The water trampoline has been blown into a tree. One of the space heaters has been upended and thrown, like a javelin, into the pool. I look into the Jacuzzi, where someone has dumped all the betta fish. They have boiled and are floating at the top like bright blue ravioli.

No one else is awake.

When I get to Noah, he is sitting up in bed, tears forming two glistening rivulets straight down his olive skin. "Noah!" I say. I'd never seen him cry before.

"I tried to call you," he says, as I hug him. "I think I saw sex."

"No, Noah. You didn't. You didn't see sex."

"Well, I think I heard sex."

"People were wrestling, Noah. It was part one of the party games. Wrestling."

"Oh. I tried to call you."

"I know, Noah. I'm sorry. I'm so very sorry."

I hug him, and he is warm and flushed from sleeping in his red fleece sweatshirt. "What do you say we go get Zoe and get out of here?"

"Affirmative," he says, forcing himself back into the robot consciousness that protects him from this messy life. "You smell like hot dogs."

I'm so pissed at myself for falling asleep and letting my guard down.

I tell Noah to tie my scarf around his eyes, so he won't witness anything untoward as I search every room in the house. We make our way across the soggy grass to the boathouse.

I can sense before we even enter it that it is empty. We sidle our way along the narrow wooden slip on one side, trying not to disturb the life jackets and fishing gear hanging on the wall. The agitated green waves in the rectangle where the boat used to go jump up at us like snapping sharks waiting to be fed. We climb the spiral staircase that leads to the whitewashed deck on top, walk out onto it, and look at the amusement park across the lake.

There, across the two hundred yards of water that separates us, we see something emerge from the mist. A black shadowy form with long dark hair. It is dressed in flowing garments that blow horizontally in the wind like flags. The shadow raises its black winged (ponchoed) arms when another streak of lightning crackles and buzzes across the sky. It seems to ignite the garlands of colored amusement-park lanterns. They seem to begin to glow.

The carousel, as if pushed by the wind, makes one slow, full rotation. The rocket swings whiz around, centrifugal force pushing them far from their center axis. A roller coaster car, stuck perpetually at the apex of the largest hill, makes one final click. The sound of its rushing descent is drowned out by an echoing clap of thunder. And then it is dark.

“Zoe!” Noah cries. We jump up and down on top of the boathouse waving our arms like castaways on a deserted island. The figure slowly lowers its arms. And looks toward us. Then it falls to its knees in the dirt.

"Come on!" I say and grab Noah's hand. We scramble down the staircase and make our way to a plastic pedal boat that's been overturned and stowed away for winter. I flip it over slowly, revealing the white and jaundiced grass now home to squirming earthworms, and drag it to the water. I throw a life jacket on him, and we pedal and pedal, but the waves and the wind make our work inconsistent.

When we get to her, she is revived and squatting on the end of the amusement park dock like a gargoyle. She is drenched. Her clothes shine and cling even more tightly to her tall, elegant form. Black watery smudges of mascara encircle her expressionless eyes and whisk down her face like Chinese characters. Wordlessly, she gets in the boat, puts Noah on her lap, and pedals with me back to Ethan Drysdale's house.

I should have never left her alone with him. I should have heeded the rumors.

But I can tell she doesn't want to talk about it, so we don't.

When we get back to the dock, and we disembark from the rocking pedal boat and hoist it out of the water, Zoe sits on the bottom step of the boathouse stairs to catch her breath. She has her head in her hands, and she stares at the ground and begins dovening back and forth a little.

"You're dovening," I say.

"I am?" she asks, finally looking up at me.

"Yes."

"It's soothing, I guess. I see why people doven." She shivers.

"Let's get out of here, Zoe," I say, gently guiding her to standing by her armpit. "What happened? Did he hurt you?"

"Who?" she asks absently.

"What do you mean, 'who?' Ethan."

"Oh," she says, dismissing me with a shake of her head. "He's nothing. Men are rats . . . Fleas on rats . . . Amoebas on fleas on rats," she quotes from *Grease*, which my mom made us watch with her a hundred times in her good days. She looks at me then, eyes bright behind the mascara tears, and says, "Hannah?"

"Yes," I say.

"They're back."

COPING

I don't have to ask, "Who's back?" because I know what she is talking about.

The-thing-that-shall-not-be-labeled (bipolar disorder) often comes with visual and auditory hallucinations.

We, the two of us, have developed a system for keeping it all in check. It's a stupid system, because we were ten when we developed it. And it probably needs to grow and change. But I was in my Pippi phase, and Zoe, when manic, acted exactly like Pippi. So when the doctors told her she has this thing, then I said, "Well, if you have it, then Pippi Longstocking has it too," and that's how we developed our system.

It was when her father left for the last time. I was sleeping over at her house. We were in her room playing. Zoe had promised to let me choose the game after a quick round of "fashion designer," and she was pinning me into a taffeta skirt.

We heard the hushed voices in her mother's room beginning to escalate into threatening barks. We heard a bunch of stuff slide off her mother's dresser and hit the floor in a crisp, clonking avalanche. We heard a body slam against the wall. We heard her mother whimper and then another thud. We heard the sound of a face being slapped with the back of a hand. Then we heard a car peeling out of the driveway.

When I turned to look at Zoe, her face was business as usual as she continued to adjust the taffeta around my waist. She hadn't even noticed that she had stuck three pins directly into the cushiony meat of her left thigh. Two-year-old Noah sleepwalked into Zoe's room, and she put some earmuffs on him and tucked him into her bed.

It was the next day when she showed me the tracks on the ice.

We were sitting on the frozen lake in our snow pants pounding a hole in the black ice with the pointy heel ends of our skate blades.

"Can I show you something?" she asked.

"Sure," I said. I had almost cracked through to the bottom, and the hole beneath my skate was filling up with water.

"You can never tell anyone," she said, and she made me blood promise, so I knew it was serious. I picked a scab, and she squeezed her chapped lips, and we mixed the blood together with the tips of our fingers.

She looked at me, trying to decide if she could trust me.

Yet her face was like a shiny tight balloon dying to burst with the news. "I . . ."

"What?" I asked her. I had no idea what could possibly be so hard to tell me. It had to be big.

"Maybe I should show you first," she said. "Get up." She held her hand out to me and hoisted me off the ice. It was like a cold desert out there. Or the moon. Everything was gray, white, and black. Like an Ansel Adams photo turned on its side. A strong breeze skimmed over the surface of the ice, blowing the snow into new shape-shifting formations. Still holding my hand, Zoe skated with me over the smooth black part of the lake—our scraping skates sounded like someone sharpening knives at Thanksgiving—until we got to the gray, opaque bumpy part. It was difficult to keep your balance over the bumps, but Zoe and I were expert lake-skaters, practicing pretend Olympic freestyle routines for hours at a time every weekend.

"Can you see it?" Zoe asked. We skated around in a bumpy circle following what seemed like the tracks of a snowmobile that had done a 360. It was the shape of an enormous bumpy snowflake.

"Snowmobile tracks?" I asked.

"No. Something else."

"What?" I had known from experience that this was probably just clumps of snow that had frozen in place on the ice.

"A spaceship," she said. "And I met them."

"Who?" I asked.

"The extraterrestrials. They taught me their language and told me they'd come back."

"When?" I asked.

"I don't know," Zoe said, looking toward the sky. We heard a big thud and boom then—the sound of the ice shifting at the fault line beneath the lake. It sounded like God cracking his knuckles.

It was after that day that everyone noticed some changes in Zoe. She couldn't control her impulses, and there was a lot of lashing out in school. She would forget where she was and speak out of turn. Teachers couldn't control her. She took a lot of risks. Jumping off her roof and onto her trampoline. Stealing her mother's car. Hooking up with boys while the rest of us were still playing Barbies. She felt invincible and superhuman sometimes and just acted on it. She thought she knew more about everything than anyone. I was her only friend.

But then she'd come crashing down. When she realized she wasn't who she thought she was, she'd get so ashamed. Her self-worth would plummet. She'd go on long crying jags and wouldn't want to leave the house.

To help her, I shared my Pippi idea. It was very simple.

If she was feeling too much like Pippi Longstocking—thoughts racing, larger than life, egotistical, invincible, frenzied—if she was feeling these things, she'd wear short stockings (socks), reminding her to slow down. She'd actually move in slow motion like she was doing tai chi or walking through water, but to everyone else she seemed to move at a normal pace. She trained herself to talk more slowly during these times, one word at a time, so that she was understood.

If I saw the short stockings, I'd remind her that she couldn't *really* pick up a horse. She couldn't *really* jump out of a moving car. She's human. Not superhuman. If she didn't recognize a Pippi episode coming on, and I noticed it before her, I would hand her some short socks that I always kept in my backpack.

When she was feeling the opposite, depressed and imagining dark scenarios that were far from the truth, when she felt like cement was filling her veins and she could barely get out of bed, she'd put on long socks, reminding her to be more like Pippi.

I'd see the long stockings and know to cheer her up. I'd remind her that her sad thoughts weren't true. Things were good and not as bad as her thoughts were making them seem. And with this simple system, we had avoided the aliens and hospital visits and the lithium—stardust, Zoe called it. She hated the stardust.

We avoided it together until three years ago when she was fourteen. Zoe threatened to hurt herself, and that was the last straw for her mom. She checked her in at a mental hospital.

The next day Zoe had to stand in line to use a *pay phone* like *One Flew Over the Cuckoo's Nest* or something.

"I can't have shoelaces. Or clips for my hair." Zoe sighed into the phone. "They watch me go to the bathroom. So I pee standing up like a guy, just to freak them out."

I didn't know a lot about those places, but what I'd gathered from TV shows is that you should probably play by the rules. "The more you play by the rules, the faster they'll let you out of there," I told her. "Why no shoelaces?"

"They think I'll hang myself with them."

"Oh," I said.

I could feel the weight of Zoe's sadness on the other end of the line as she whispered, "Just a minute," to the crazy lady behind her waiting to use the phone.

"When can I visit?" I asked.

When I got there the next day, Zoe was sitting on a couch in the lounge, reading a magazine. She'd crafted a braided, turban-like headband out of her pillowcase because they wouldn't let her have barrettes.

The hospital walls were painted in muted tones of puce—the color of tongue and bologna. Those inspirational posters they sell in airplane magazines that define words like *Success* and *Responsibility* in corny ways hung in strategic locations. A spindly anorexic girl sat at the occupational therapy table in the corner gluing the Serenity Prayer to a wooden plaque with the dry noodle letters of alphabet soup.

"Are you being have?" I asked Zoe, using the special syntax we made up for *behave.*

She nodded and said, "Except I'm not taking these." She held out a handful of pretty pink pills, like tiny Easter eggs, that she'd managed to hide beneath her tongue at meds time. I grabbed them from her and shoved them in my pocket.

"The shrinks don't like it when I talk about them, but they're real," Zoe said.

"Who?" I asked.

"You know who. Aliens," she loud-whispered.

"If you want to get out of here, you maybe should stop talking about them."

"What should I tell them, then? They won't let me out until I say something."

"Do they have arts and crafts or something?" I had imagined it like a big summer camp.

"Uh-huh."

"Draw some hearts and rainbows, write happy entries in your journal. Eat, even when you are not hungry. Always agree with them."

"Okay."

"And sit down when you pee."

"Aww, that was fun."

"Zoe," I said.

"Okay."

I looked her in the eye. And it turned into a staring

contest. Zoe tried to make me laugh by crossing her eyes and sticking out her tongue, but I'd seen *that* a million times before, and I persisted, examining the turquoise part of her eyes and moving to her pupils to see if she'd closed them off to the world. But she hadn't. She seemed back to normal. No need for all this incarceration business. What she needed was to stop acting like Pippi. Adults did not understand kids who acted like Pippi.

A bell rang, and the nurses started kicking people out. I hugged Zoe, her chickeny bones poking through her sweatshirt. She wasn't eating or sleeping much, which was part of the thing that she had: the-thing-that-shall-not-be-named.

"Guess what?" I'd said to her.

"That's what," she answered.

"No, guess what for real."

"What?"

"You're going to get better," I said.

Then, Zoe being who she is, said, "'The final, and only, act of healing is to accept that there's nothing wrong with you.'"

"Okay," I said, looking around for the poster she must have been reading it from, but it wasn't there.

"There are aliens, and they did speak to me. I am okay with you not believing that. But that is my reality."

"Okay," I said.

"Don't judge me," she said.

"I don't," I insisted. "But we just have to smooth things over with the overlords on this planet, parents, teachers, et cetera, so that this doesn't happen again. The lockup. We can't be having it. Agreed?"

"Agreed," she said, and we did our secret handshake.

Visiting hours ended. Mothers said their tortured, guilty good-byes. Siblings, relieved to get the hell out of there, lined up at the heavy locked door of the unit like puppies waiting to pee. I joined them with my mom, who had been waiting for me near the nurses' station.

We left, and when the door, heavy as the hatch of a submarine, sealed itself between me and Zoe, the depth of this situation washed over me and left me gasping for breath. I turned to take one more peek through the tiny window, and I saw Zoe in the hallway, crying, collapsed, and crumpled into a ball as if someone had tossed her into a wastepaper basket. The nurse guided her to her feet and led her to her room, holding an ominous glinting needle in the gloved right hand behind her back.

"No!" I screamed. "She doesn't need that!" I pounded on the door. My mom tugged at my elbow, and then I saw a Cyclopsian security camera staring right at my third eye. I remembered to keep my composure or they'd lock me up too.

That was three years ago. And that's the last time I heard the *A*-word.

Until last night.

When I took her home from Ethan Drysdale's house, I was hoping she'd sleep it off, but this morning when I came over, I found her in the basement, and it looked like she'd been working for twenty-four hours straight.

She is in constant motion, scuttling between piles of silks, jerseys, corduroys, satins, and velvets, her mannequins, and her sewing machine. She grabs a voluminous bundle of bright pink tulle spun like cotton candy and glides to the sewing machine. She has pins in her mouth and scissors in her back pocket. A measuring tape around her neck. Her hair is in a tousled ponytail that is becoming one large matted dreadlock. Her eyes are red.

I've seen her like this before.

"Try this on. I need to see how long to make the sleeve."

"Zoe, what is going on?"

"I started a new collection," she says quickly. Her thoughts are fast. Too fast for her mouth to keep up with them, so she stops trying to talk, waves her hand around, and points to the rack against the side wall, which is bowed in the center from the weight of what's hanging on it.

The collection relies heavily on some old black three-quarter-sleeve concert T-shirts with cutouts that are laced together with ropes of silver chain. These are paired with tailored velvet leggings the bright-white colors of lightning: white-orange, white-blue, white-lilac. They have intricate, jagged seams and are matched with fitted feminine velvet jackets whose sleeves taper at the wrists and end in fingerless gloves. The tulle is for petticoats beneath full, cloud-colored skirts. A charcoal evening dress seems to smoke and swirl around its subject like a tornado, the collar orbiting around the mannequin's head in a theatrical hood.

"It's good," I tell her.

"I know." She finishes her seam and rips the thread from the bobbin with her teeth. "I made a new installment for Noah too. It's about hunger-slash-desire. He has to know how to access it. He has to know what he wants. It's good to want things. We should know what we want, but society takes away our hunger. At least it does for girls. It takes away our hunger. Our desire. And tells us to be quiet and skinny and supportive. That's the way it goes. If-you-can-be-skinny-and-quiet-and-supportive-you-may-even-get-on-TV-while-you-watch-from-the-sidelines-as-your-husband-wins-a-golf-tournament."

She says all of this without taking a breath, zips the final skirt around the waist of her headless dress form. Her eyes are a little off-kilter and glassy. One seems a tiny bit bigger than the other, and her pupils are strangely dilated. Crazy eyes. Her fingers are in constant motion.

"Maybe you should brush your hair," I say in a complete role reversal. "Maybe we should talk about last night. It seems like something happened. Zo. It seems like you're working something out. What happened?" I hug her, trying to compress her body and slow it down. I look down, and I notice she's not wearing any socks at all.

"It's not going to work anymore, Banana," Zoe says, reading my mind. She wiggles her bare toes at me.

"Then we'll think of something else," I say.

ELATION

It's Sunday. I called over, and Zoe's mom Susan said that she was asleep. It is a deep, worrisome kind of sleep, though. No one is able to rouse her at all. Noah has been climbing on top of her, tickling her nose with a feather, spraying her with a water bottle, to no avail. Susan is keeping close tabs on her. I decide to let her sleep.

I should set up the hot dog cart and try to make some sales, but I do need to think, and I do that best at the lake. So I go to the beach and sit on the bench at the end of the parking lot peninsula. I turn my head toward the sun, close my eyes, and listen to the lake as it laps and licks at the rocks.

I relax, and I try to replay the moment that Danny Spinelli bolted for the stairs at Ethan's.

Did he really say, "Call me"? Or was I dreaming? I replay it over and over again. "Crap," he said. "Gotta go." He was blushing. His legs could have taken the entire staircase in one leap, but he floated up two at a time. He was afraid to get caught with me. And he fled. Taking the steps two at a time, and he said . . . *Call me.*

Or maybe he didn't.

Maybe I wanted him to say that.

I force myself to think about something else. Honestly, in a million years, even if he *had* said, "Call me," would I do it? No. So it doesn't matter. What matters is that Zoe is in bed. And I can't get her to talk about it. That should be my focus.

I try to think of a new cognitive behavioral therapy device (this is what the shrinks call it), like the socks, that will jog her into controlling her moods.

"I didn't think anyone ever sat on this bench," says a voice.

I turn around and jump when I see Danny Spinelli leaning on a piling, his arms crossed in front of him, studying me. His infinite legs are crossed too. I wonder how he can find pants that fit him so well.

"That is one stealthy ice cream truck. I didn't even hear you," I manage to say, hoping my voice sounds breathy and ethereal but knowing it is actually nervous and pinched and nasally. "Um. I come here to think," I tell him.

"What are you thinking about?" He sits down next to me, and we look out at the lake.

"Cognitive behavioral therapy. You?" I actually flip my hair. I wish Zoe could have seen it.

"Whoa. That's deep. Now I don't want to say what I was thinking about."

"What?" I insist.

"Never mind," he says, blushing. "You should never ask a guy what he's thinking. Ninety percent of the time he's thinking of unbuttoning your blouse. The other ten percent is just blank. Or filled with the occasional thoughts about food. But only when we're already starving and cranky."

"You're not giving your gender much credit. I mean, you did get a lot done while you had us enslaved, barefoot, and pregnant for most of history. You had to have had a few other ideas."

"Nope. That's pretty much it. It's pretty motivating." He nervous-yawns and stretches, wrapping his legs over top of each other and landing his elbow on the seat back. Shy, graceful, and catlike. It's beautiful, the way he moves.

"I should wear more buttons," I say with a sigh.

Danny stares down at me, smiling. "What?" he asks me, poking me in the rib.

"Nothing," I say. I will never wash this rib again. "You kissed me once," I say.

"I remember."

"You do?"

"Of course."

I don't think he remembers it the way I remember it, though. For me it was a perfect moment.

Somehow, a big group of us ended up at the beach. Boys and girls together. It was a day like today. Crisp but not cold. Sweatshirt weather. Danny's sweatshirt was red.

A game of Nerf football started, and we ran around like a whirling rainbow of sweatshirts and Converse sneakers, and I caught the ball. Danny, his hands too big for him even then, grabbed me and pulled me onto the autumn's dying grass. He looked at me, and without hesitation pressed his wet, red lips against mine. It was so instantaneous and unpremeditated. Time stopped. I felt relaxed. Contented. At home in myself. And for a microsecond of eternity, it was like we were in the Garden of Eden.

We had that kiss. And after that, I began to understand the story of Adam and Eve. The falling from grace. It was as if Danny's impossibly red lips were the apple, and after I kissed them I was never again comfortable inside my own body. Something clamped around my stomach and my throat. I was suddenly ashamed and constantly aware of the fact that I was being watched. I no longer just *did* things; I wondered what I *looked like* while I was doing them.

He smiles, shakes his head as if he were remembering it too and needed to jolt himself back into the present. "Can I buy you an ice cream?" he asks. "I know a place." He points to the spot in the parking lot where he has left the truck.

"Do you have a Toasted Almond?" I say.

"Whoa, that's old school. And with all the nut allergies these days, I can't risk it. I have SpongeBob, or Spider-Man with gumball eyes, or if you want something with actual milk and sugar in it, you'll have to go for an ice cream sandwich."

"Perfect. I enjoy ice cream sandwiches."

Danny gestures in a gentlemanly way for me to walk in front of him. I'm shivering from having dipped my toes into the lake or from suddenly being on a "date" with Danny Spinelli. I shiver again and almost flutter a little like Noah would. Danny wraps his hoodie around my shoulders.

When we get to his truck, he jumps inside and digs around in his deep coolers for an ice cream sandwich. I never realized that there were so many muscles on top of one's shoulder. They bulge through the soft cotton of his T-shirt as he pushes around his product in search of my old-school ice cream sandwich.

"Okay. Here we go." He hands it to me, and I unwrap it.

"Want some?" I ask.

"No," he says, leaning his forearms on the edge of the service window.

I'm proud of myself for taking a small girly bite and not wielding my tongue around the edges, which is what I would normally do. A speedboat buzzes like an annoying insect across the lake.

"Remember the story of the guy . . ."

"Yeah," I say. I don't need him to finish it. There was

the story about the guy who was decapitated during the annual speedboat regatta. He flipped his boat at 200 mph, fell out, got run over by another boat, and was left with his head bobbing and floating in the water like a cantaloupe. There was also the one about the guy who fell through the ice in his snowmobile and the one about the girl who wandered home alone from the carnival and got murdered in the woods. And the legend of the hopefully vegetarian sea monster that had the head of a moose and the wrinkled gray body of an elephant. Small-town, lake-country lore designed to keep kids terrified and on land and close to home.

He unwraps a Bomb Pop, and we walk together along the beach letting the edge of the water slip beneath our sneakers.

He smiles at me, feeling the same elation I am, I can tell. I can tell because the feeling hangs between us like a rope. When you share a feeling with someone it takes on matter and weight. Even if you're the only ones who can sense it, it becomes a tangible thing with properties like shape and weight and heat.

"You like it here," Danny says. "On the lake."

"I guess. It feels like part of my body," I say. "It's hard to explain. Leaving would feel like an amputation in a way."

"But it would be cutting off the part that hurts," Danny says, throwing a rock into the water.

"Exactly," I say. He gets me. "But I would still miss it."

"Want to see *my* favorite place to think?"

"Sure," I say.

The old playground by the beach has not been updated since the seventies. It's still made of metal and cement, so kids can still scrape their precious knees and get a few stitches, which is good for them, I think. Sometimes being poor is good. You learn coping skills.

"This is it," says Danny, and he points at an enormous scratchy cement tube some construction workers thought would make a good play structure along with some old tires and splintery railroad ties. It's tagged with a red spray-paint heart. He crawls in and sits down, puts his feet up on one side of the tube, and bends his legs into his chest. "I don't really fit as well as I used to. Come on in," he says.

I hate myself for doing it, but I *Seventeen* magazinerize this moment:

> *When a guy asks you to join him inside an enormous cement pipe with no one else around, do you: A. Crawl in next to him, ignoring the fact that he has a girlfriend. B. Tell him you have to go. C. Call the police.*

I've been waiting for this moment for six years, so I choose A. His enormous feet are straddling a window-like hole in the cement that perfectly frames the pale disc of the sun. My athletic left quadriceps is grazing his, and I think I might spontaneously combust. Luckily it's cool inside the pipe, so I feel the blush on my face turn from fuchsia to carnation pink.

"See how it blocks out the outside world?"

It is silent. The constant chatter of the universe is finally quiet for once. I take a deep breath and remember what that feels like. Breath. It seems like I've been holding mine for a long time.

Danny places his hand on the knee of my brown corduroys and traces my patella in wide concentric orbits. I put my hand on top of his, and he flips it over, using that magic index finger to follow the lines inside my palm.

"You read palms?" I ask him.

"Indeed," he says. He brings my palm closer to his face and shakes his head, *tsk*ing.

"What?" I ask.

"You are a hard worker," he says, tracing a line at the inside of my wrist.

Like sands through an hourglass, my insides are draining through my core.

"That's what I like about you," he continues. "You try. Not everyone is like that." His hand finds the waistband of my sweatshirt and moves up beneath it. I am not wearing a bra.

"That's not my palm," I tell him.

"Don't worry, it's part of the process," he says.

"Really," I say. "I'm suspicious."

He leans his long torso over and kisses me then, pressing

his lips softly against mine, taking gentle nip-like kisses until I open my mouth.

I am immediately in love with him. As if touching tongues was the final step in some ancient magic ritual.

I try to think of Zoe stuck in bed, her hair matted against her face, or my dad drinking at the end of the bar, or Rebecca Forman's bad teeth. I think of her posse of cheerleader friends who wouldn't be afraid to beat the crap out of me. That does it, and I break away, remembering to suck in a little like Zoe taught me. The sign of an expert kisser.

"I have to go," I tell him.

"Okay," he says, and I love him even more for not pressing the issue. His lips are wet and red and glossy. His cheeks are flushed. And he looks at me, shaking his head like he doesn't know what to do with me. He likes me, I think, but I push it out of my mind.

We crawl out of the pipe, and walk back to my bench. A pair of mallards flies low and furiously over the surface of the lake.

"They mate for life, you know," Danny says.

"Because their lives are short," I quip.

"You're a glass-is-half-empty kind of girl, aren't you?"

"No, not really. I just like surprises, so I keep my expectations low."

He seems to think for a moment and then says, "The difference is subtle."

LUST

Zoeeeeeeeeeeeeeeeeeeeeeeeeeeeeeeeeeeeeeeeeeeeeeeeeeeeeeeee eeeeeeeeeeeeeeeeeeeeeeeeeeeeeeeeeeeee, I text.

But she doesn't respond.

She won't pick up her phone. It's killing me.

There is such a thing as a shy extrovert. People think extroverts are all loud and mouthy, like Rebecca Forman, but that's not true. The definitions of *extrovert* and *introvert* have to do with how you process the world and from where you draw your energy. I'm shy, but I process my world by talking about it. Which makes me an extrovert. But I don't talk about it with just anyone. I have to talk about it with Zoe.

Zoeeeeeeeeeeeeeeeeeeeeeeeeeeeeeeeeeeeeeeeeeeeeeeeeeeeee eeeeeeeeeeeeeeeeeeeeeeeeeee, I text again.

My retelling of events to Zoe is what grounds them, shapes them, makes them real. If I can't tell Zoe about kissing Danny Spinelli, it didn't happen.

I call her mom to find out what's going on.

"Susan," I say.

"Hannah."

"What's going on?"

"Well."

"Well, what?"

"Well. She promised to let me watch her for a week. If she doesn't get better, we're going to the hospital."

"So it's like an S-word watch?" We never say the word *suicide* out loud.

"No. We're not there yet."

"So it's like a what?"

"Just a watch. I'm watching her." Susan had quit smoking years ago, but I hear her exhale what can only be cigarette smoke from the side of her mouth, then I hear some *tamp-tamp*ing into what must be an ashtray. I trust Zoe's mom because she's a nurse and she sees so much *humanity* on a daily basis. She usually understands people, especially people in crisis, and knows what to do about it.

"Should I come over?"

"Why don't we let her rest?"

"Okay . . ."

"Don't think I forgot about the fact that you two took Noah to a party. I'm going to visit that at a more appropriate time."

"Okay," I say, and I hang up.

For that entire week Zoe is on lockdown and doesn't even go to school. I text her, but she doesn't answer.

So for an entire week, I worry about her. And without her counsel, I have to pretend I didn't kiss Danny Spinelli. I avoid him, sneaking through the halls and eating my lunch in the library, because I don't know what to say to him.

For an entire week, I sneak alone to the attic at Sussex Country Day. (The secretary notices me, but she turns a blind eye.) She and my mom used to play bridge. I learn the conditional past tense in Spanish and how to find the volume of a curve when you rotate it around its axis. Two things I will never use. I watch Ethan Drysdale stare catatonically at the whiteboard. He doesn't remove his sunglasses. Which would never fly in public school. And he doodles in his notebook, what seem to be large storm clouds and crooked flashes of lightning.

I go alone to sell the hot dogs, reading in my chaise lounge as the *whoosh* of the highway relaxes me and covers me in gray dust.

I go alone to my father-who-is-back-on-the-wagon's AA meetings, and I whisper the Serenity Prayer along with the drunks.

God grant me the serenity to accept the things I cannot change
The courage to change the things I can
And the wisdom to know the difference.

I try to be supportive, wearing my EASY DOES IT, ONE DAY AT A TIME T-shirts and making random Crown Royal sweeps through his cupboards and filling his refrigerator with fresh vegetables and grapefruit juice (a natural detoxifier).

I learn to accept my fate. Accept the things I cannot change. For a whole week, my life is pretty calm, the way I like it. Huddled among the soft weeping of old men in the dark basements of churches.

And then on the seventh day, I go to Zoe's house. It's Friday morning.

I go into her room, and she's still in bed. The dreadful black poppies of the mock-Marimekko comforter, which she made herself, wrap around her body, as if strangling her. Her feet, still bare, stick out from the bottom.

I walk to her side and lift her limp arm off the bed. Gravity pulls it back to the mattress.

"Zoe. Get up," I say, but she won't budge.

"Draw me a picture," she mutters into her pillow.

"Of what?" I ask.

"Of why I should get out of bed."

She's made bedroom furniture out of found objects like milk crates and button boxes. Underneath a table made out of a stop sign, I find some printer paper and a Sharpie. I begin to draw.

"Don't do flowers and rainbows."

I crumple up the paper and get another one. This time I draw a huge rippling staff of music filled with notes and an electric guitar.

"What's that?"

"Music."

"That's enough."

"That's enough drawing?"

"No, that's enough to live for. Music."

"See? Then get up."

"I just need five more minutes," she says, and she rolls back over.

"Zoe . . . Zo," I say, but she's already fallen back to sleep.

I go back to the front door. Noah's on the stoop reading when I ask him how he is.

Without looking up from his book, he says, "You know I can't answer that question, so why do you ask it, Hannah? I can answer where I am, and who I am, and what I am doing, but I cannot answer the question how I am."

"I want you to know that Zoe'll get up soon, okay?" I say, as I hug him close and muss his straight hair a little. "Because whether you know it or not, you are probably feeling frightened by the party, and lonely without Zoe to take you to school. You probably miss your routine, and I want you to know it will all fall back into place. Okay?"

"What I feel without Zoe is lonely?"

"Yes."

"What is it that I feel for you right now because you told me that?"

"Gratitude, perhaps. Or friendship."

"Is friendship a feeling?"

"Not necessarily. I guess what you feel for friends is a special love."

"Does not compute," Noah says in his robot voice, and he lets out a rare Noah giggle and smile.

I start to get up to go, and he holds out his hand to stop me. "Will you bring me to school, Hannah?"

"Where is your mom, buddy?"

"She's crying a lot because of Zoe. Sadness-slash-despair again," he sighs.

"I'll take you," I say. I yell into the screen door that I have Noah. I hear Susan blow her nose, and then she yells, "Thank you, Hannah."

"And don't do anything rash," I yell. "Zoe will be fine." I'm not sure about this, but I don't want her sticking Zoe in the hospital again.

"I'm giving it one more day," she says.

Taking Noah to school is not part of my routine, and I begin to feel the agitation, a tingling in my hands and feet and my chest closing up like a vault, that happens when I veer from my habitual schedule. I don't have time to stop at the corner store for my corn muffin. I don't have time to take the long way past Danny Spinelli's house. I won't have time to give my first-period homework a once-over. I won't have time to park in my regular parking spot.

This makes me a little testy with Noah. But he can't pick up on it anyway and continues to speak at me about the different categories of star.

"Okay, I'm going to quiz you now. What color star is the hottest?"

I haven't been listening, but I try, "Blue."

"Good job," he says, and luckily we pull up to his school before he can ask me another question.

He opens the door and flutters out of it before I can say, "Have a nice day," and before he can close the door, Danny Spinelli grabs the top corner of it and holds it open. He has a little sister Noah's age, and he must have been dropping her off.

"May I?" Danny asks as he slips into the passenger seat and slams the door.

"You already have," I say. His knees fold up almost into his armpits, so I show him how to pull up the lever and send the seat back.

"You've been avoiding me. Want to go for a ride?"

"Now?"

"Yeah. No one cares if I miss school as long as I'm back for practice."

My palms are freezing and sweaty at the same time, and my stomach twists and cramps. These are not cute physical manifestations of first love but, sadly, my anxiety about missing a day of school. I never have missed a day of school. Even when people seemed to stop keeping track of attendance, I continued to show up every day. "I can't miss school," I tell him.

"Why?" he asks.

"I just can't. It's a thing with me."

"Can I talk you down?"

"You can try."

"Okay, so relax your grip on the steering wheel and take a deep breath in through your nose. Good. Now, slowly release the breath as if you're blowing through a straw . . . We are going to miss school today, Hannah." The timbre of his voice vibrates at my center, and I relax for a second, but when I hear "miss school," I tighten my grip again, and my shoulders hunch up toward my ears.

"Boy, this is harder than I thought," he says.

"It's a personal goal of mine," I say. "Perfect attendance."

"Perfect should never be a goal. Perfect just happens if you let it."

"Whoa."

"You learn that from sports. Perfect happens only if you get out of its way. So what time do you need to be there for it to count as a full day?"

"Ten," I say.

"That gives us plenty of time."

"For what?"

"Turn left. Take 206," he says.

On the drive through other country parts of New Jersey, horse farms and rolling hills and woodsy big estates, I wonder what the hell happened to make him suddenly so interested in me. There must be a rumor circulating that I gave someone a blow job. That's the only way I can possibly explain it. It's a perfect linear equation. FALSE BLOWJOB RUMOR = SUDDEN UNEXPLAINED ATTENTION FROM BOYS.

"So is there a rumor circulating about me?"

"What do you mean?" he asks.

"Well, you and I don't usually hang out," I answer.

"Yeah. I'm trying to change that."

"Why? What about Rebecca?"

"I'm tired of them."

"Who?"

"*Everyone.* You know, that's the word they use to describe themselves. They consider themselves *everyone.* 'Everyone's meeting at the beach.' 'Meet us at the mall. Everyone is going to be there.' Everyone who matters in their universe."

"I'm not part of everyone?"

"Not usually, no. That's what I like about you."

"That's what you like about me now. Until you start to miss 'everyone.'" I don't even ask if he's broken up with her. Somehow I don't feel like I have the right. Like it's none of my business. Because I could never understand what they have together.

"Don't do that."

"What?"

"Try to discredit what I'm saying to you. You have to know that I've always liked you. Since second grade when we sat across from each other and you taught me that trick about the nine times table and you let me copy your answers."

"I just wanted to help."

"And that's what I like about you."

"That's not very romantic. Those are the same feelings you have for a preschool teacher."

"Stop. Pull over. We can be real with each other. You and I are, as they say, cut from the same cloth."

"Aren't you and Rebecca 'cut from the same cloth'?"

"I think what we had has run its course. We're bored with each other."

"And so you've set your sights on me? I'm not the most exciting person in the universe. I sell hot dogs."

"You're going to make me prove this to you, aren't you? Look at me. You are one of the hottest girls in school. And you're smart and ambitious and kind. Which none of those others are. You are the only girl worth pursuing. And that's why no one pursues you. You, Hannah Rose Morgan, are intimidating. These losers know they could never live up to what you deserve. And the only reason you don't know how physically beautiful you are is because you're always standing next to Zoe. Who, granted, is hot as hell, but she is not relationship material."

"Watch it. That's my best friend," I say. I'm smiling, incredulously. Does he really expect me to believe that I have no boyfriend because I'm too good for "everyone"? I look him in the eye and shake my head.

"You don't believe me."

"No," I say.

"Fine. You forced me to do this," he says. "We're sitting here in a gas station parking lot at eight thirty in the morning, and just the idea of being next to you in a car has done this." He reaches over, grabs my unmanicured hand, and places it on top of the button fly of his extra-tall boot-cut jeans.

The thing beneath it is rock hard, alive, and insistent. I pull my hand away quickly and giggle. "That seems happy to see me," I say.

"It is."

"From what I've read, though, seventeen-year-old male parts are happy to see anyone. Or it could happen just from driving over a bumpy road."

"What have you been reading?" He laughs. "That's fourteen-year-old male parts. Seventeen-year-olds begin to discriminate. I like you, okay?"

"I like you too."

"Really?" he says.

"Always have."

"Okay," he says back, and when he smiles, his eyes crinkle up a little on the sides. It is so adorable, I want to spend the rest of my entire life trying to make him smile. We drive about three more country miles until he directs me to a remote, hilly, and abandoned driving range with Canadian geese grazing among white clusters of far-off jettisoned golf balls.

"I never fancied you a golfer," I tell him.

"I'm terrible at it. But of all the sports on the planet, it's the best at teaching you to get out of your own way. To find perfection by quieting your mind."

"Ha. Sport. Golf is not a sport."

"What are you talking about?"

"If ninety-year-old ladies can play it, it's a game. Like shuffleboard. Or pinochle."

He stares at me for a second and smiles. The crinkling happens again, and I am rubbery. How is this happening to me? For a second I think of Zoe and wonder if she's gotten out of bed. I think of telling Danny about it, but I want to stay positive. That's what she would tell me to do. I forcefully push Zoe out of my mind so that I can hit golf balls with Danny Spinelli while we're supposed to be at school. I know how to hit a golf ball. So I have to decide whether I let him show me or whether I try to impress him. A difficult choice. But then I think maybe I can do both.

Someone has left an old rusty driver sitting in a canister to the left of the shack where you would buy baskets of balls in the summer. He grabs that and runs out onto the grass, collecting balls and shoving them into his deep pockets. When he returns, I let him show me how to swing, so that he can touch me. He stands behind me, and together we hold the club. The insides of his smooth forearms graze lightly against the backs of mine, and my arm hair stands on end. He lifts the club behind us and presses against me as he shows me how to turn my hips. Then he kisses me on the neck, which unbeknownst to me until this very moment is an intense erogenous zone for Taureans, especially those born in April. We don't even hit an actual ball before we're back in the car, kissing in the backseat in broad daylight. Finally I come to my senses.

"We need to go. This is moving too fast. I'm missing school. Rebecca . . . We need to go," I say with a sigh. Danny lifts his face from where it was nestled in my chest and looks at me. "Now," I say, stroking my finger down the bridge of his beautifully slightly crooked nose. When I get to his lips, tracing them gently, he takes my finger in his mouth. I pull it out with a pop because it really is going too far. "We have to go," I tell him.

"You're killing me."

"I'm sorry."

"Okay." He hoists himself off me, and I take a deep breath.

We straighten out our clothes, get back into the front seat, and start driving. We stop at 7-Eleven and get Big Gulps, mostly full of ice, so Danny can hold the cup in his lap for the rest of the drive to school.

On the way there, he talks about his enthusiasm for the food truck industry. And I realize that we don't actually have a shared passion for mobile restaurantrepreneurship (Zoe's word for what I do). I'm doing the hot dogs because my sexist, tight-as-a-clam's-ass father won't pay for college for his girl-child.

Danny is doing it because he loves it. He tells me that he's read all of Colonel Sanders's biographies. "Colonel Sanders tried to sell his Original Recipe idea more than a thousand times before he had a taker. Business is all about persistence," he says. "And optimism." Then he actually quotes something from Henry Ford. "'Whether you think you can or you can't, you're right,'" he says, and then adds hesitantly, "Right?"

"Right," I say. "Words to live by."

He's brave, I think. *He cares*, I think. And I care too.

Not about hot dogs specifically, or food trucks, or the Original Recipe, but I feel that I care deeply about vague things that haven't yet crystallized in my heart.

NATURE

According to her texts, Zoe is now up and showered. She assures me she'll be at my house tomorrow bright and early to share with me the epiphanies from her dreams. Things sound like they're on the up and up, but you never quite know for sure with Zoe.

On the phone I go through our checklist:

"How is your mood?" I ask her jokingly, because that's what they would ask her every day in the hospital. "Have you lost interest in your favorite activities? Are you participating in risky behaviors? Irritable? Sleeping too much or too little?" I slip in there: "Talking to aliens?"

"Just needed some rest," she says.

I try to take her word for it, until I see for myself tomorrow.

In the meantime, Danny's enthusiasm for mobile restaurantpreneurship motivates me to hitch the cart up and make some sales after school. The rec league has late soccer practice, and if you want to sell some hot dogs on a weeknight, you just have to follow the minivans. I take the dusty dirt road to the field behind the supermarket and set up next to a little pond.

It's two days until Thanksgiving, and it still hasn't frozen. The ducks even forgot to fly south. They swim along the ripply frosty edges of the water, puffing out their chests, daring us to ask them to leave now, when the daffodil shoots are already poking their razor-sharp leaves out of the dirt. The kids are still playing in their T-shirts. Nature, it seems, is seriously out of whack. So it is completely in tune with my life.

I put on my baseball hat with the pink and yellow logo in which HANNAH'S is spelled out in one continual cursive chain of linked-together sausages—Zoe designed it and had it silk-screened on some hats and aprons for my birthday—and I get busy marrying the ketchups and boiling up the water. For the kids, it's all about the ketchup.

I've made friends with some of the regular moms. By regular moms I mean both the fact that they buy hot dogs from me regularly and the fact that they're not too pretentious to let their kids eat the occasional hot dog. They're also not too uppity to be seen talking to a teenager. They're the kind of mom I hope to be. I like the ones with senses of humor who realize not everything has to be perfect.

My favorites are Karen and Jen. They both sit next to me on lawn chairs as I set up the cart. They're drinking from ergonomic, BPA-free water bottles, but I'm certain they are not filled with water.

"I'm bored," Karen says. She's wearing her mom uniform. Tight black yoga pants that don't breathe because of the tummy-control panels, and a perfectly highlighted ponytail. "Tell me what's happening in the wild life of Johnson High," she says. "Are you just 'sexting' the whole day long? . . . CHLOE!" she interrupts herself, yelling toward the field, "Stop doing cartwheels in the midfield!" then without missing a beat resumes her conversation with me. "I sent a naked picture to my husband the other day, and he had his phone sitting face up on the table in the conference room. His boss totally saw my boobs."

"Karen!" Jen says. These two are kind of like me and Zoe in the future. Karen is the Zoe one. "I'm sorry, Hannah. She is *so* embarrassing. Filter!" she says to Karen. "Where is your filter?"

"Don't you get tired of the filter? We have to use it all day with the kids. A woman can never speak the truth. So. Tell me, Hannah. Who do you have your eye on?"

"Don't answer her, Hannah, just so she can get her rocks off. She is disgusting."

I only pause for a second. I need to tell *someone*, and Zoe has been MIA. "Actually," I say as I drop eight franks into the boiling water and shut the lid. They both lean closer to me. "Do you know Danny Spinelli? With the ice cream truck?"

"Get. Out. Of. Town!" says Karen. And then, "SHOOT! JACKSON!!! He always putters up close to the goal and then forgets to get a shot off . . . Danny Spinelli?!?"

"He's adorable," says Jen.

"And how big are that kid's feet, like size fifteen?"

"My god, you are disgusting. Hannah . . ." she begins.

"Size matters," Karen interrupts. "Don't let her convince you it doesn't."

"It doesn't," Jen says to me, and then, "Hey, I'm sorry about your dad. That must be hard."

"Um, my dad?" I ask. As far as I know he's been going to meetings and drinking the grapefruit juice for weeks now. But everyone in the neighborhood knows about his issues. He's the closest they all have to a town drunk. "Oh, I guess you didn't see," Jen says, blushing.

"And now who needs a filter, big mouth?" Karen says to her and then motions her fingers across her lips as if she's zipping them up. "Don't worry about it, pussycat," she says to me. "It's just a little publicity. And you know what they say about publicity. All publicity is good publicity."

But this I know cannot be true. I'm too embarrassed to ask them to spell it out for me, so I try to focus on selling at least the eight hot dogs I've cooked before packing up furiously and driving home.

In my room, I rip open my laptop, google his name, and there he is. On YouTube.

It's from last night's weather report. In the video, he is obviously drunk, his nose lit up like the clown that he is. And he is having a public breakdown for everyone to see. "I'm drunk," he's telling his audience. "And you know why I'm drunk? First of all, because I can perform this stupid job inebriated," he slurs. "But mostly because these people won't let me tell you the truth. The truth is that we're screwed, and it's too late to change anything because we've done irreversible damage to the climate. Because stupid-ass politicians won't listen to science but pander to their idiotic constituencies. Because of some idiots who believe that everything in the Bible really HAPPENED, we are now headed the way of the dinosaurs. Ashes to ashes. Oil to oil.

"That wind outside, people. That is not a normal wind. I've never seen anything like it . . ." He burps, and then the producer finally cuts to a commercial for trucking school. Which seems tempting to me for a second. I like to drive. I've probably made enough money with the hot dogs to go to trucking school.

In the next link, they broadcast his forced, public apology: "And I hereby rescind my statement that the oil companies, one of whom owns this television station, have completely run this country into ruin . . ."

It's hard to say what I feel about this. I am numb with disappointment. And shame. I pull out my phone and call him, but he's not picking up.

I start clicking away again on the laptop, because it suddenly occurs to me I should check some things. I can feel a hot liquid terror rising through my body like mercury in a thermometer. I start furiously clicking away, paying what I can online from my mom's account, before he can figure out a way to drain it. Mortgage, electric, car insurance. This begins to calm me down. Putting things in balance.

It was two years ago when I started paying the bills for my mother. Things just started getting shut off. Gas, and electricity, and landlines. So I told her to give me all her passwords and account information, and I took over. I'm good at it. I enjoy a nice spreadsheet. It's clean and pure. Nothing can hide in a spreadsheet. Which is why, realistically, I'm thinking a career in accounting.

I write checks for the rest, signing her name in the perfect cursive they used to teach people in grammar school. I enter it all in a spreadsheet that makes satisfying cash-register noises when I enter a deduction. Reluctantly I open my own account for the hot dogs.

It's in the red. Twenty-seven fifty in the red. I hope I'm wrong, so I shut it down and reboot it. There was $2,466 in there yesterday. I take a breath and let the truth of the matter wash over me, but I can't believe it. I slam the laptop closed, yank the cord from the wall, and hoist the computer out the window, letting out some kind of primal animal sound in the process. A roar? A squeal? A cry? A bellow. I think I bellowed.

He took it all.

I find him at Mickey's, and he's still half in the bag. An old slang term for *drunk* that I learned from my AA friends.

"You should call your sponsor," I tell him in a flat monotone.

"Sorry about the money, but I lost the job, and you'll have to kick in to support the family," he says. "That's how it works—" He takes a last sip and slams his glass down on the bar. "In families."

"Is it?" I say. "I wouldn't know."

"Oh, so now this is about you. Poor *you*," he mock-whines, contorting his face into a grotesque red monster.

"Call your sponsor," I tell him. I'm numb with fury.

"I said I was sorry. AA teaches you that."

"No, you didn't, actually. And I wish AA would teach you not to fuck up in the first place. Then we'd have something."

"Watch your mouth, young lady," he says, raising his hand to me.

This, for some reason, makes me laugh. I laugh until I'm doubled over, and my friend Obey, the ancient German shepherd guard dog, comes over to sniff at me and figure out what's happening. I laugh until tears start running down my cheeks, and I keep laughing until I can't tell if I'm laughing or crying. Obey licks my face. I try to catch my breath, and stick my fingers into the dog's thick winter coat. I squat down and hug him around his enormous brisket while he keeps licking away my tears.

My body seems to move on its own after that. I am not inside of it but watching it move more fluidly than it usually does as it hitches the hot dog cart to my car and drives it to the boat launch by the beach. I do a three-point turn with the rig, which is no easy feat, and then I back it up to the cement ramp and I lower it slowly into the lake. First the mini tires, then the propane tank, then the chrome box with the diamond quilting effect on the side. The mini grill for toasting buns, and then the pans for the hot dogs, sauerkraut, and relish. I get out and wade around back in the frigid water to unhitch the cart.

It releases with a heavy metallic thud, and I watch Hannah's Hot Dogs roll deeper and deeper into the water until the only thing left to see is the yellow umbrella, which I left open. A little deserted island of what was left of my hope. "Fuck you!!!" I scream at it until that too, gets slowly consumed by the waves.

I sit numbly on a bench and look out to the lake, and I'm reminded of that story about the frog and the scorpion.

The one where the scorpion asks the frog for a ride across the river. The frog is suspicious at first. "Why would I do that?" he asks. And the scorpion, sharp as a tack, responds, "Because if I sting you, I will die too." That makes sense to the frog. He's eager to please, because that is his nature, so he decides to give the scorpion a lift.

The scorpion stings him, in the deepest part of the river, because that is in *his* nature, and together they sink to the bottom.

"Bad day in the food service industry?"

I can recognize his voice by the way it lusciously vibrates through my body. I don't even have to use my ears.

"Never mix business with family," I tell him without turning around. "What are you doing here?"

"Saw your car," he says and comes to sit next to me. "Do you at least have insurance on that thing?"

"Doesn't matter. I've given it to my higher power. The lake. Is my higher power."

"That's supposed to be a metaphor, right? You're not actually supp—"

"Have you broken up with Rebecca?" I blurt.

"Well, I was . . ."

"Don't."

"What?"

"Don't break up with her. You don't want any part of this," I say, swirling my hand in the air. "I don't mean to be presumptuous or anything, but you seem to be testing the waters. And these waters are seriously polluted. With scorpion venom and Crown Royal and all sorts of toxic whatnot. Stay with Rebecca."

"But—" I hear him say as I get up, get into my car, slam the door, and drive away.

Back home, I sit on the end of the dock letting the scratchy rough edges of the two-by-fours press into my calf meat. I just want to feel something, and this does the trick. For a moment I can understand the inclination of cutters.

The pain soothes me, and the lake soothes me, too. I can see how other people would find it creepy and dark—would be afraid of what lurks beneath the surface—but I've grown up with it. I can't imagine living without it. To me it is soothing, and blue and clear. A baptismal font. A big life lozenge living in my backyard. Looking at it literally slows my heartbeat.

A muskrat, slick and black like oil, floats back home to its nest beneath the neighbor's dock. It ignores me and my problems, which I try to remind myself are First World Problems. Number one, nobody died. Number two, I'm not orphaned or starving. Number three, no one sold me into sex slavery. Number four, I do not live in a landfill.

I try to put things in perspective, despite the whiny Zoe voice inside my head that keeps interrupting. "But who steals hard-earned college money from a teenager? Who *does* that?" it asks.

My father, I guess, does that.

I try to think of the story Danny told me about Colonel Sanders. How at the age of ten his father died, so he was shipped off to another farm to work and raise money to support his family. And when he was fired for, like, being *ten,* his mom shamed him mercilessly and shipped him off to another farm to try again.

No one sent me off to work on a farm.

And if they had, it would make me stronger. Colonel Sanders got strong and famous and finger-lickin' good at everything after that. So, this is a test.

But I didn't have to push Danny away. I don't know why I did that. The pain of that finally sinks in. I'm without him. I'm worried about what to do about Zoe. I slide slowly, toes first, scraping my whole body against the dock, as it slithers soundlessly into the frigid water. I let it envelop me like an amniotic sac. And when I burst free, breathless, I hope I can figure out how to start over.

FREEDOM

Inside, my mom has left a note on the kitchen counter, as if it suddenly mattered to me where she was. "At the gym," it says, and then, "On a date!" *That's wonderful*, I think somewhat sarcastically and head to my room to change and try to stop shivering.

I walk right into my closet without turning on the lights. I strip down, peeling off my wet clothes. I throw a towel around myself and sit at my desk. I erase the entire Wiener Meter and draw a new black outline of an empty hot dog.

"Why is the Wiener Meter set to zero?" says a voice behind me.

I spring out of my seat and back myself into my bedroom door. Zoe is sitting on my bed, her long legs tied into a jegging-colored pretzel. Her hair, a matted black curtain, hangs in front of her face as she tries to untangle it a strand at a time.

"What the hell are you doing here?! How did you get in?" I ask her.

"The fake rock. With the key in it. You should maybe scatter some other rocks around it. It looks a little conspicuous sitting out there by itself. What happened to the wieners?"

"Nothing," I say. "What happened to the long nap?"

"I woke up."

"Did your mom let you out?"

"Define *let*," she says.

"It's a three-letter word for *allowed*," I say, wrapping my freezing hair into a towel turban.

"I allowed myself out, I guess," she says, paging through a magazine I left near my bed. "Why are you soaked?"

"No reason. Rebooting, I guess."

And then she explains how before she snuck out for a cigarette break—

"Cigarette break? You don't smoke," I tell her.

"Everyone smokes on the inside," she says, as if her bedroom were some kind of prison, and then she tells me how before she snuck into the woods during a cigarette break from her suicide watch, she turned her room into an intangible-thing installation: an exhibit on freedom. She wrote the Bill of Rights on a roll of toilet paper, carved the Statue of Liberty out of a bar of soap. Drew the DON'T TREAD ON ME snake on one of the walls, and folded her sheet, origami style, into a bald eagle. She hoped her mom'd ponder that and start to treat her with more respect.

"She was trying to help you, Zoe. How did you get here?" I ask her.

"Hitched," she says, sticking out her bony thumb and pulling it to the right. "Karen and Jen picked me up. Those two are nuts."

"Okay, well, we should tell your mom where you are," I say. I stand up, walk over to the bed, and hold my hand out to help her up.

"No, I can't deal with her right now. She doesn't get me. You get me, Hannah. She just wants to keep me in a box. She thinks if she can box me in, I'll someday become like her, and Karen and Jen. I can't be like them. It's not that I'm crazy; I just have slightly bigger ideas than most people."

"It's okay to have big ideas," I tell her. "'It's okay to have two dads. It's okay to eat macaroni and cheese in the bathtub. It's okay to be small, medium, large, or extra-large . . .'" I continue, quoting from our favorite picture book that we read to Noah when he was little.

But I've been doing some more reading about bipolar disorder. The grandiosity. The inflated self-esteem. And the paranoia that can sometimes accompany a manic phase. The suicidal depressive stuff. I'm learning that it might not be "okay to be bipolar" unless you're on medication.

"Maybe you should go talk to someone, Zo. A doctor."

"Doctor? Don't you remember last time? If I had one idea of my own, they'd call it noncompliance and then take things away like showers and phone calls. My IQ is exponentially higher than every one of the doctors' and nurses', and yet they would control my entire fate. If I cried one tear out of frustration, they'd label me 'depressed' and increase my medication. It's barbaric, Hannah. What I need . . ." she says, hanging on to the last syllable so I can tell that she wants something from me.

"What?" I ask her. "What do you need?"

"Don't let them make me a lab rat, Hannah. I need to get out of here."

She is getting agitated again, and she stands up and begins straightening all the stuff on my shelves. My books, my trophies from third grade, my matchbook collection.

"What do you mean, 'out of here'?"

"Road trip. You need one too, obviously. Your life is in the shitter. Everything gets better when you get out of town."

"I need to deal with some stuff here," I tell her.

"I saw the video. That's exactly *why* you need to get out of here. You need to stop rescuing his ass. Let him figure it out for himself this time, Banana. Plus . . . everyone will be talking about it at school."

"Well played," I tell her. She knows how hard it will be for me to face the people whispering about me behind my back. If she wants me to get out of town, that's the reason I would go.

She gets up and hugs me, and I cry a little onto the shoulder of her T-shirt.

"Your shoulder bone just poked me in the eye bone. You're doing the not-eating thing."

"I don't need food right now. I need to get out of town. Till after Thanksgiving. That should be enough time."

"Enough time for what?" I had forgotten about Thanksgiving.

"Stuff," she says.

"Well. This is bad timing. There were some developments. In the Danny Spinelli department. You slept through them. I had to talk about it with the soccer moms."

"I'm listening," Zoe says.

"Things were going well, and then I kind of sabotaged it." I pace back and forth with my forehead in my hands. "And I can't miss school tomorrow. I have a math test, and the school newspaper is going out. So we'll have to deal with your shit here. In town. Because I have shit to deal with too."

Zoe finds a nail file in my drawer and begins scraping it against her thumbnail. "'Why think about that, when all the golden lands ahead of you and all kinds of unforeseen events wait lurking to surprise you and make you glad you're alive to see?'" she asks distractedly.

"*Walden*?"

"Nope. *On the Road*. Jack Kerouac. I memorized it."

"The whole book?"

"I have newfound abilities."

"You need to talk to someone. You said yourself, the

socks won't work. It's sort of stupid to think that they would keep working."

"Fine. I know what I need to do. It came to me while I was sleeping. I need to hit the road, and I'll go with or without you."

"Fine, go," I say, waving her away.

"You're calling my bluff."

"It's okay to call someone's bluff."

"No it's not." Zoe says, sticking out her bottom lip. "Hannah. Come with me. Please," she begs. "Just for a little while. We'll go talk to Danny right now. I'll explain to him you'll be back in a day or two. What harm could forty-eight hours do? You've been waiting to kiss him for six years. And . . ."

"And what?" I ask.

"And she signed the papers."

"What papers? Who?"

"My mom . . . The commitment papers. She's putting me in."

"No. I told her not to, Zo . . ."

"Well, she's like a mom and a nurse, and you are a seventeen-year-old hot dog vendor. She probably felt like she didn't need to consult you."

"She really did it? Are you bullshitting me?" I'm astonished and hurt that she didn't talk to me about it.

Zoe unravels some documents she'd folded back and forth into a paper fan.

"Fuck," I say.

"Now you're talking. Pack a bag," she says. "We're going on an insouciant adventure. Insouciance. That's your first intangible thing."

"I don't need intangible lessons," I say. "I feel things."

"Yes. But you feel the wrong things. Trust me. We're leaving now," Zoe says. "Packy packy!" She sweeps around the room looking for a bag to put some of my stuff in.

I think of him while I smooth out and fold the ice cream sandwich wrapper he gave me and tuck it into my back pocket. "I think I can smell that he likes me. Danny," I say. "He smells different. There's a depth. You know how the lake smells different where it's deepest?"

"The lake has a smell?"

"Oh my god, do you notice *anything*?"

"I notice that you think you can smell water, or that you can smell *love*, for that matter, and I am the one they think is crazy. Anyway, it was bound to happen, you and Danny. But this is unfortunate timing. Because I have to go."

I throw some things in the bag. My favorite jeans, a T-shirt, some underwear and a toothbrush, my phone charger, the shampoo that's supposed to "volumize" my hair. Also, *The Brothers Lionheart.* I pretend it was written for me.

"What will we do for money?" I suddenly realize. "As you can see, the hot dog money has been depleted."

"Of course it has. By him, right? And I'm sure you've already forgiven him."

"Having a resentment is like drinking poison and expecting someone else to die." It's a quote from AA.

"Whatever. Your father makes me feel good about not having a father. That's what a jerk he is."

"Yeah, well, he's still my father, so it hurts my feelings when you say that."

"The coins," she says.

"It's come to that?" I ask.

"It has."

Deep in the bottom of her closet sit two heavy boxes of coins that her grandmother, because she doesn't know about Coinstar, rolled all by herself, every night for two years while watching *Jeopardy.* Two thousand dollars worth of coins. Zoe and I were saving it for an emergency, and I guess this qualifies.

We go to her house first, and sneak into her room. The first box rips a little as I drag it out from her closet by a lid-flap. It is graffittied with Magic Marker sayings like BREAK GLASS IN CASE OF EMERGENCY, RESULTS MAY VARY, DON'T TRY THIS AT HOME, OBJECTS IN MIRROR ARE CLOSER THAN THEY APPEAR, MAYBE YOU SHOULD WEAR A HELMET.

Zoe stares at it as if I'd just pulled a giant squid out of the ocean. "It's really come to this?" she whispers.

"Well, yeah," I say. "We're kind of running away."

We each hold one heavy box of coins as we waddle our way to the car and toss them into the backseat well with a satisfying *thud.* At least the coins will weigh us down if we get into a fender bender with an SUV. We settle in the front seat; I adjust the rearview and back the car out of the driveway.

"I didn't get in to Parsons," she admits with a sigh.

"Oh no." I look her in the eye.

"Or FIT."

"But if only they could see your new stuff . . ." I say.

"Too late."

"I just registered at County. They have some design courses. You could come with me." But I try to imagine her there. At a commuter college, where she is smarter than everyone in charge but too oblivious to know her place. Nothing good could come of it.

"County jail . . . County College. Same thing," she says as she looks beseechingly toward the sky. She's still clutching a corner of the cardboard box flap that ripped off the coins, and she begins to stroke it lightly across her wrist. "We. Are. Better. Than. That." One stroke for each word. *Better* gets two strokes in an X. She believes this with a conviction rooted deep in her gut. I know because I can feel it. I can feel her feelings sometimes, like she can read my thoughts. It's as if we're some kind of Siamese twins connected at the soul.

I reach for the box flap and gently take it from her before it can break the skin.

A strange gusty wind blows through the open window, and her hair stands straight up and then whips across her face in satiny ribbons. She looks out the window, and a fat raindrop splashes onto her cheek, then she looks at me. "That's a sign. We have to go," she says, urgently. "Let's say good-bye to your boyfriend. I'll give you ten minutes."

HEARTBREAK

I drive to Danny's while Zoe pores over an old road atlas and creates playlists on my iPod at the same time. She's talking to herself, but only a little, and waving what might be hallucinatory flies away from her face.

His house is an old converted mobile home in a neighborhood called Sun Valley or "Scum Valley" if you're lucky enough not to have to live here. It's your typical white ghetto with rusting car parts on the front lawns, underwear on the line, last year's dead Christmas wreaths still hanging on the doors.

I hear the music coming from the half-light of the small basement window near the ground. A deep thudding, like the rhythm of my heart.

His mom works hard, when she can get work, and she's working now at Casa Bianca, a gourmet restaurant, possibly mafia owned because no one can figure out why they'd put it here except to launder money or feed gangsters after they bury their debtors in the woods.

There's a heaviness inside me as I peer at that window and imagine him inside. I want to be with him there, underground forever, and melt with him into the earth. I've never felt so heavy and deeply rooted. I want to grow roots and vines from my body and ensnare him forever in my branches. No wonder we scare men away.

As much as I'm feeling a density and gravity and rootedness, a deep pulling need to stay and absorb him into my body, Zoe is feeling the opposite. She is feeling the flighty lightness from the adrenaline of her escape. "Come on," she says from behind me, pushing me through the door. "I'll give you fifteen minutes. Enough for a quickie."

"Right," I mutter. I tiptoe across the foyer toward the entrance to the kitchen and take a left down a dark hallway. It is home to a gallery of sepia-toned, sun-damaged school portraits of Danny and his sister at ages five, six, seven, and eight. I study him. It's strange how he looks exactly like himself. How everything, the crookedy nose, the crinkly-eyed smile, was there from the beginning, just waiting to reach its full glorious Danny potential. I find an open door after "DANNY, AGE 8," and it leads to the stairs of the basement.

"Hello," I say into the doorway, but he can't hear me over the music. "Danny," I say a little louder.

I start down the stairs, sliding one hand down each wall as I go. I am about to bend over and peek beneath the ceiling of the finished basement when I hear it. It's quick, but it is a distinct slurping, spitty inhale—air whistling around too many teeth, followed by a short nasally goose honk. Rebecca's laugh.

I think maybe I'm hearing things. Maybe it's just some improvisation in Jimi Hendrix's *Blues* blaring from the stereo. I stay where I am on the stairs, but I get the courage to dip my head down so I can see into the dimly lit basement.

I see an old indoor basketball hoop arcade game surrounded by a net. I see an entertainment center along the wall with an old stereo and an even older television. The speakers on either side vibrate with the bass. I see a few basketball trophies on the windowsill, and then I dare to look at the plaid, skirted pullout couch along the wall . . . and there she is.

She has her feet on the couch with her knees bent up on either side of her, exposing her crotch to the room. Her crotch is clothed, though, in tight dark-wash jeans that come just to her pudgy hips.

She is very comfortable here. It is her couch, says her posture. The couch she and Danny have christened. And she sits like she has a right to it. There is no awkwardness. No wondering what Danny thinks of her. No newness to this relationship. It runs deep, and I suddenly don't know what I'm doing here.

The intense anticipatory throbbing that I was feeling beneath my diaphragm and in my nether regions begins to climb. It moves up and pounds against my rib cage. Then it climbs higher and strangles my throat. It finally lands behind my eyes, where it stays and threatens to make me cry.

I let out a gasp and run up the stairs.

I keep running out across the sharp crackling thirsty dead grass and across the street to a wooded lot, where I bend down and try to catch my breath.

"Hannah, what's wrong?" Zoe asks. She was sitting on the stoop looking at a road atlas with a tiny magnifying glass.

"Nothing." I can't breathe. It feels like I've run twenty miles.

"What, Hannah?" Zoe places a hand between my shoulder blades.

"Nothing," I say. A tear squeezes itself out of a tear duct, and some of the pressure is released. "Nothing," I say again.

I know I told him to stay with her, but I guess I didn't think he actually would. My shock and sadness take on cosmic proportions. I can feel my heart spin, getting denser and denser until it turns inside out on itself, leaving a black hole in the center of my chest. I wish Noah were here so I could describe it to him. "Let's get the hell out of here," I say.

Zoe, because she experiences them (sometimes all in the same hour), understands the full range of human emotions. She is very sympathetic on the first leg of our trip. She lets me cry for a while, then buys me an Oreo Blizzard at Dairy Queen before we officially hit the road.

"Open up," she says, trying to feed it to me with the big red plastic spoon as we sit in the DQ parking lot.

I shake my head like a toddler refusing strained peas.

"Come on, Hannah, it's a Blizzard. It'll make you feel better. Want some whipped cream on it? Wait. I'll go get you some whipped cream." She gets out of the car, pops the plastic lid off the Blizzard and then tilts it toward the cashier and points to the top of it. "Whipped cream," I hear her say, and then she hands her two extra quarters that she peels from our first roll of emergency coins.

She hands me the cup, and I take one bite. It does make me feel a tiny bit better. The cold is soothing the lump in my throat.

"So you're crying for two reasons," Zoe says. "The first one is because your dream is squashed, and that's a valid reason for crying. The second is because you feel like a fool. And that one is not valid. You deserved him more than anyone. You deserve better than him, obviously, if he gave up on you so quickly. He is the fool. Not you. Say it out loud," she says as she wipes my tears with a scratchy DQ napkin.

"What?"

"He's the fool."

"He's the fool," I mumble through my whipped cream.

"No, say it like you mean it."

"He's the fool."

"Now yell it out the window."

"He's the fool!" I yell. But a new tear comes to my eye, because Danny is really not a fool at all. He's smart. And grounded and ambitious and hardworking. Like a perfect working-class Jerseyan hero in a Bruce or Bon Jovi ballad. And I'm the one who pushed him away. *I'm the fool*, I think.

Zoe thinks I've recovered enough to start driving, though. And I'm really ready to get out of here too at this point. Who cares if we ever come back. Really, all those great songs about New Jersey were about getting the hell out of it.

INSOUCIANCE

Zoe has an idea for the first stop on our adventure, and it requires getting to Exit 13A on the Jersey Turnpike. Believe it or not, we don't know how to get to the Jersey Turnpike from where we live. We've never been on it. Even on the rare occasion that we drive to New York City, we take Route 80 east. If we go to the shore—which we rarely do because we live on a huge lake that provides us with our summer entertainment—we take the Parkway. The turnpike, she is mysterious to us.

We hear she is mostly gaseous, like Saturn. And that the gases swirl around you in fluorescent ribbons. We hear it smells like propane and pickles and manure, a vinegarish primordial swamp.

And the rumors, they are true enough. We find the turnpike in spite of having turned off our phones and the GPS. Zoe says we need to be entirely off the satellite. Off the grid. In case they start looking for us. She even makes me rip off the E-ZPass detector on the windshield. We'll have to pay the tolls with our coins, listen to FM radio or sing to ourselves.

After we pass Newark Airport and I try to race some of the landing airplanes in my old LeMans that's shaped like a roller skate, I see where Zoe is probably bringing me: IKEA. The closest we can get to Sweden on the New Jersey Turnpike.

It looms ahead of us, a bright blue and yellow beacon surrounded by flags. Something solid among all the gas. Land ho. "Is that where we're going?" I ask Zoe.

"How did you guess?"

"We don't really have room in the car to bring anything home," I say.

"We're not bringing anything home. We're going to make this our home. Just for a night."

"We're sleeping here?" I had heard of people having dinner parties at IKEA just to see if the kitchen they picked would suit their lifestyle. IKEA is like that. It wants you to try things out. It wants people to be happy. It wants you to believe you *have* a "lifestyle." It also fosters self-reliance. You pick your own stuff, you check it out, you build it. You take responsibility for your own design. "I didn't know they let people sleep here," I say in a dreamy sigh.

"Define *let*."

"It's a three-letter word for *allow*. We've been over this."

"Sometimes you just have to take what you want. Park over here in the corner so no one will see the car."

"No, Zoe."

"Trust me," Zoe says, staring at me.

"Have you read the diagnostic symptoms for bipolar disorder? You're flagrantly displaying some of them."

"I'm not *flagrantly* doing anything. I could actually be a lot more flagrant. I am showing some restraint, actually. And you need to be more flagrant. You need to be flagrantly insouciant. You care way too much. And because of that you will be paralyzed for life and miss out on everything. Please. Open the door and de-LeMans. Our first lesson is Insouciance."

We walk across the emptying parking lot beneath the swooping, even at ten at night, gulls. They peck at discarded chicken bones on the pavement, grab some, wave them around, and then toss them aside.

"Look at them," Zoe says. "Do you think they care about making a mess of the parking lot? They just get their needs met and move on. Insouciant."

A plane lands on the other side of the highway and drowns out the competing noise of the road. We sneak into the exit door beneath this blanket of sound and are immediately comforted by the panacea of a climate-controlled box store. Away from all the movement outside, the kinetic energy. Inside, everything is still and solid. Furniture can at least be depended on for that.

Most everyone has left the building, and the management

is flashing the lights and asking people to bring their purchases to the self-checkout lines. They have already turned off the big escalator that leads up to the showroom. We sneak into the heavy doors of the Marketplace and follow the arrows on the floor that lead us to the warehouse. We wind through a maze of dishes, pots, Tupperware, utensils, garbage cans, textiles, pillows, lighting, prints, frames, candles, and plants. In the textile section we hide behind some shower curtains, and Zoe, as if she's the Ghost of Christmas Present or something, points to a couple taking their time deciding on a bathroom rug. Their backs are turned to their three children, who are cackling and throwing pillows all over the floor and jumping in their dirty sneakers from big pile of rug to big pile of rug.

"Do you think they care that their children are destroying property?"

"Obviously not."

"Because they came here to get a bathroom rug, and this is the only time they have in their busy schedules to get a bathroom rug, and they can't afford a babysitter just to go out and buy a stupid bathroom rug, and so they don't really give a shit about their kids tearing around the store or the employees who will be late getting home because they can't decide between the tangerine or the electric blue."

"Insouciance?"

"Yes. It's the art of not giving a shit. And you need to foster some of it."

She's right. It's true that I care too much. Things stick to me and I cannot shake them off. And so I should stop caring. Insouciance. Go F yourself.

An IKEA employee in a yellow polo shirt saunters over and asks the couple to make their choice and make their way to check out. He picks up a juice box and some crushed Goldfish that the rogue children have left on the floor and shakes his head.

Zoe and I slowly and quietly step back so you cannot see our sneakers beneath the row of shower curtains. Zoe holds her finger to her lips as if I needed a reminder to keep quiet. Her shower curtain has patches of transparent plastic in its design, so she finds a clear spot and smooshes her face against it, trying to make me laugh.

When the final customers pay and leave, we hear the employees lock the doors, and someone turns up the stereo. I wish it were *Take a Chance on Me* by ABBA, just to complete my Swedish experience, but it's not. It's Green Day.

We wait for some yellow-shirted, potbellied blokes to sweep through our department with a push broom, and when the lights turn even dimmer, the stereo turns off, and the intermittent employee chatter subsides, we sneak out from behind the curtains. We still don't talk, but Zoe signals me to follow her in silence. We sneak like soldiers toward the staircase that leads up to the cafeteria. Zoe runs, hunched over, to a corner, looks around, and then signals for me to follow her. Eventually we slingshot this way to the stairs. We stay close to the wall in case there are cameras in the center of the stairway and sidle our way up.

We practically crawl behind the chrome tray rails to the kitchen part of the cafeteria. Zoe pulls open a big stainless steel freezer and points into it. Bags and bags of Swedish meatballs. She finds me a plate, dumps about twelve of them out, and sticks the whole thing in the microwave. She only heats one plate. She takes it out before it beeps and very quietly narrates what she's doing in "Swedish Chef" language ("snerkin smorkin snerkin smorkin") as she scoops some lingonberry jam onto the plate, with a little parsley for garnish.

We take the plain, utilitarian, ceramic plate to the tables along the windows that overlook Newark Airport, and we watch the planes landing in the dark. Sometimes they seem to materialize from some other dimension. They seem invisible. Just rows of lights until they suddenly hit the ground and hurtle down the runway at impossible speeds. While we watch, some streaks of lightning flash through the bleak polluted skies of Newark and Elizabeth, illuminating their far-off urban landscapes.

"Uh-oh," Zoe whispers. "I thought I had more time."

"For what?" I whisper with a meatball still stuck in my cheek.

Zoe just shakes her head and looks off into the sky.

I am devouring the plate of meatballs, and I keep offering them up to Zoe, but she won't eat them. I am begging her to take the last meatball. It sits happily on the end of my fork like an upside-down exclamation point, and I fly it toward her mouth like a mom feeding a toddler. Finally she takes the whole fork from me and jams the meatball in her mouth. She's chewing it with difficulty when someone says, "Stop right there," in a scary old-man voice. "What the hell are you two doing here?"

We freeze, deer-in-headlights style.

I am about to run. But Zoe turns on her faux-calm, smooth-everything-over voice. The one my mom used to use when she called the pediatrician's office.

"Hello." She stands up and looks at his nametag. "Hello, Officer Franz. Apparently no one told you about tonight's inventory. We start at midnight," she says, pretending to look at the watch she's not wearing.

"Oh, no. There's no inventory tonight. I would have known about that." Officer Franz has white hair. His pants are pulled up almost to his chest. He's wearing comfortable, black rubber-soled shoes, and I think he may be packing. A Taser at least.

"It was called at the last minute, with Black Friday approaching and all. Maybe you forgot," Zoe says sweetly. "Hannah, you just stay there, and get started while I show Officer Franz the memo. I think Officer Franz is getting very sleepy, aren't you?" Zoe says. I see her walk him around the corner as he yawns. She guides him toward the mattress department and then returns three minutes later.

"He's asleep," she says.

"What did you do, read him *Goodnight Moon*? You can't just put a grown man to sleep."

"He was really tired, I guess. Anyway. Here we are. What do you want to do first? And don't you dare clean up that plate. You leave it there. Insouciance, remember. Tonight we do not care."

I look down at the plate, glistening with brown gravy and magenta lingonberry goo. And I force myself to throw my napkin on top of it and walk away.

The first thing we do is plan our future interiors. We saunter through the showroom. I pick an avocado kitchen with a glass tile backsplash. Zoe picks one with dark wood cabinets and cherry-red accents. We circle the entire showroom, making our choices for each room, until I'm ready for bed too. We brush our teeth in the public bathroom and then snuggle into a four-poster bed called Leirvik. I am tempted for a moment to move to the bunk beds across the room, but I choose the four-poster because it seems romantic, except for the name of it.

I settle into my Leirvik bed with Gäspa sheets and a Gosa pillow. Zoe lies next to me. She's pretending that she's going to sleep with me, but I know she'll sneak away as soon as I drift off. I can still feel her manic energy radiating off her in hot waves.

I want to enjoy my IKEA experience, but I feel like a dead flower. Like someone has drained the nectar of youth from my soul and left me brittle and old and ready to snap.

It physically hurts to think of Danny, and I can't stop visualizing the scene in the basement. I'm so disappointed in myself for sabotaging it. If there was even an "it" to begin with. A tear slides out of the corner of my eye, and drops onto the pillow.

"You're not being in-sou-ci-ant . . ." Zoe says in a faux warning tone of voice.

"I can't help it." I sniffle. "I'm so embarrassed by it all. Does this ever happen to you?"

"No. It's not like that with me."

"What's it like with you?"

"I just want to lure them in, and once I catch them, I lose interest."

It's true. I've seen Zoe make a catch and then bat him around a little, like a cat playing with a housefly.

"What about Ethan?" I say, proud of myself for taking advantage of the opening she left me.

Zoe just stares at me, lowers her eyebrows, and points her finger at me like a gun. "*Boom*," she says, faux shooting, her hand kicking back a little.

"See what I did there?" I say. "We were talking about

boys, so I just nonchalantly mentioned his name. Because maybe you'll feel better if you talk about him."

She tosses and turns a bit and then gets out of bed and performs a few arabesques and a split leap, completely ignoring me.

"What's with the ballet?"

"I don't know. I'm suddenly feeling it. We should have taken lessons."

"We did."

"Oh yeah."

"For three years."

"That must be why I know how to do this," she says and lifts into a double pirouette ending in fourth. "Ta da."

"*Bellisimo*," I say.

"Really, though, Hannah. This is your first heartbreak. It's supposed to hurt. You'll get used to it. Read me a story," Zoe says, and I riffle through my bag and read her some *Brothers Lionheart* before I fall asleep and the book drops, corner first, onto the floor.

In the morning she quietly lifts the comforter off me, and I pull it back on and roll into a ball on my side. "Not yet," I say.

"Now, Hannah. We have to scoot."

"Did Officer Franz wake up?" I ask.

"Well, no. He's not responding to stimuli."

"What kind of stimuli?"

"Screaming in his ear. Wet willies. Noogies. Indian burns."

"Is he breathing?"

"Yes. But we should get out of here."

I can hear the rhythmic beep of an alarm coming from some far-off part of the showroom. I wipe the drool from the side of my face and pack my things back into my messenger bag and start making the bed.

"Leave it!" Zoe whisper-yells.

We scurry out to the warehouse "pick-it" bins, and in the center is an enormous rocket-ship sculpture made entirely out of different IKEA chairs. "Did you do that?" I ask Zoe. It wasn't there last night.

"Come on," she whispers.

"Using only an Allen wrench?" I ask as I gaze at it, walking backward. Zoe is pulling me through checkout to the frozen food section. She has baked me a cinnamon roll and hands it to me as she drags me to the exit.

It's locked.

I jump up and down on the rubber mat, trying to activate the automatic door, but it won't budge.

"We need a crowbar," I say, but Zoe just sticks her hand between the panes of glass and something gives. The door slides open. We run to my turquoise beaten-up LeMans just as two police cars and a fire truck roll up to the IKEA entrance.

"Go that way," Zoe says, and we sneak out of the back exit of the parking lot and merge onto the turnpike toward New York City.

AUDACITY

The tolls are killing us. We have to use a whole roll of quarters and two rolls of pennies just to get through the Lincoln Tunnel. Luckily we ate for free at IKEA. The cinnamon bun sits like a lump of clay in my stomach and will keep me full for at least six hours.

I love how as you approach the entrance to the Lincoln Tunnel on its elevated C-curve Jetsons-like ramp, they give you a quick glimpse of the skyline before spinning you around and plunging you beneath the Hudson. You get to look across to the crystalline, pristine, pointy city twinkling like Oz and think, "In just ten minutes (or an hour, depending on traffic), I will move from *here*, where nothing ever happens that's good, to *there*, the center of the universe."

It's crowded today, the day before the big Macy's Thanksgiving Day Parade, and people are filling up the tunnel like lemmings or cockroaches running from the light, ready to infest the streets just to look at . . . what? Balloons?

Marching bands? What is the appeal? I guess it's just another place to go to take pictures of your kids. It's a Facebook opportunity. There are worse things to live for.

"Why do you want to go to the city today of all days?" I ask Zoe. It has taken me the forty-minute drive down the turnpike to accept the fact that I will miss school today and that the school newspaper will probably not go out. It's a half-day, though, so I force myself to get over it.

"I have some unfinished business," she says, trying to be tough and mafia-esque. She folds a piece of Juicy Fruit into her mouth and stares straight ahead, looking through a pair of aviator sunglasses that she may or may not have stolen from Officer Franz.

As we start to turn away from the view of the city and toward the entrance to the tunnel, our senses are assaulted by a giant black-and-white billboard for the revival of *A Chorus Line*, which is my favorite musical in the world because it is a meta-musical about a musical and because for some reason, I identify with the plight of these young people who want to believe they're special. Like Zoe. She really needs to believe she's special. I admire that about her. Because you have to believe you're special before you can do anything special.

"I think what you need is a plan for the future," I tell her now. "Let's come up with a plan and next steps, and then we can go home for Thanksgiving dinner."

"I had a plan," she says.

"You need a Plan B."

"Plan Bs are for losers."

"Is it Plan Bs or *Plans B*? Like *mothers-in-law*?"

Zoe just nods a little, smirks, and otherwise ignores me.

We have to wait longer and pay more because Zoe ripped off the E-ZPass. The toll collector's hand drops as I place the heavy rods of coins into it. She shakes her head at us, and Zoe says, "What? It's money. You have a problem with our money?" The toll taker just gives us a pathetic laugh, and we pull away.

The old decrepit brick entrance quickly gives way to the space-age white tile and fluorescent lights of the *Star Wars*y tunnel. It's as if we're being transported to another dimension. And we are, because when we emerge, we get to a place where anything can happen and sometimes does. Which may have been a phrase from an old NYC brochure we had lying around the house, but I'm not sure.

You would think driving in New York is a scary thing, but it's not. Especially in Midtown. The entire thing is a grid, so it's impossible to get lost. Especially if you know which avenues travel uptown and which down and which streets go east and which ones go west. Once you have that down, and you remember to ignore the lane lines and go with the flow of traffic, the taxis will avoid you. So you just pull in and go. Like a red blood cell traveling in a vein.

"Where to?" I ask Zoe.

"Twenty-seventh and Seventh," she says.

I turn right on Forty-second and another right on Seventh where it splits off from Broadway. It's only ten blocks, but it takes a while. Miraculously I find a twelve-hour meter on Twenty-eighth Street. But that too sucks up a lot of our precious coinage.

We de-LeMans once again, and Zoe unfurls her spidery legs, steps to the sidewalk, and grabs a kids' backpack in the shape of a green turtle shell from the backseat. She must have stolen it from IKEA, but this is the first time I notice it.

"Come on," she says, snapping her gum.

She struts up to Seventh like a tall, svelte Teenage Mutant Ninja Turtle, and without even thinking about it, takes out a spray can of blackboard paint that she must have also stolen from IKEA. She shakes it as we walk, the marble clonking around inside, until we come to the monolithic beastly home of the Fashion Institute of Technology, a solid brown brick on Seventh that straddles Twenty-seventh Street.

Zoe stops at a brass sculpture in the shape of a small skateboard ramp, topped on one side by a big elliptical donut and on the other side by the spherical donut hole. She doesn't stop to think before spraying FUCK YOU across the base. She tucks the spray can under her arm and runs. I follow after her, down Twenty-seventh until she comes to a hideous white and blue archway built in front of the student center.

The campus has emptied out for Thanksgiving, so no one sees her as she shimmies like Spider-Man up the inside of the archway and in full daylight sprays the same thing on the underside of its white hood. She lets go, lands gracefully in a squat on the sidewalk, and we run again back to Seventh, turn left, and run upstream around the tourists toward Thirty-fourth and Madison Square Garden, where we can finally duck into Penn Station and hide out underground.

We're squatting against a shiny black marble wall, trying to catch our breath. The station is shaped like an underground octopus. At the center are the ticketing booths and the big old-fashioned flip board announcing arrivals and departures. Branching out from the center are the hallways that lead to NJ Transit, Amtrak, or the Long Island Rail Road. Carved into the black marble walls around the periphery are bagel shops, pizza joints, newsstands, and random underground ethnic boutiques selling head scarves and sunglasses and incense.

"Oh my god," Zoe says. "That felt good."

"Are you kidding me? You are better than that!"

"No, *you* are better than that. I feel fantastic for doing it. Fuck them. They can't control my future. I'm too good for them."

"Zoe. I need to tell you the story of Colonel Sanders."

"Who the fuck is Colonel Sanders?" You can tell she's really amped up when she uses the *F* word a lot.

"The Kentucky Fried Chicken guy. He failed more than a thousand times with his Original Recipe until it finally worked out for him. You've only failed once. You just have to keep trying."

"That's sage advice coming from someone who didn't try at all. I need to tell you the story of Audacity. It's your next intangible thing. When someone screws you over, you need to have the audacity to fight back. Men get that. Women don't. Today, we cultivate Audacity."

I check in with Zoe's eyes. The right one once again seems a little smaller than the left. Her pupils are glassy and unfocused. I thought this trip might ground her and help her come to terms with reality, but she hasn't come back to Earth yet.

We spend some time chilling out underground at Penn Station. It's a little less crowded down here. No tourist would even think of plunging into these bowels. And most of the commuters are home defrosting their turkeys, so what's left are Zoe and me and a bunch of homeless alcoholics who smell like pee. Some of them congregate in the seated waiting area until a cop walks by and kicks them out. "Hey, go pick those off somewhere else," he says. A matted-hair woman wrapped in her shelter-issued wool blanket stands up, still scratching as she shuffles away in her flip-flops.

I think about my dad, happy that at least he's never gotten this low. Something keeps saving him before he completely destroys his life. He has some hope left.

Zoe ducks into a boutique and steals a fire-colored scarf, which she wraps around her head.

"That is not inconspicuous," I tell her.

"It's audacious, though, word of the day," she says and continues walking through the station like she owns the place. On her travels through the hallways, she is not only audacious but resourceful enough to gather the tools she apparently needs for our next adventure: a Swiss Army knife, some black wool caps, a Polaroid camera, and two long, puffy down coats to use as sleeping bags. These she gets by begging some matronly women headed toward the LIRR. They probably have teenagers like us at home and they literally gave her the coats off their backs. At twilight she says we can go.

We wear the sleeping-bag coats, whose sleeves are too short for both of us, and fill the pockets with the hats and camera and Swiss Army knife, and we take the train to Eighty-first Street. A familiar stop for us: It's the Museum of Natural History.

"The museum tonight?" I ask her. "Noah will be so jealous. It will be like *From the Mixed-Up Files* . . ." It was one of our favorite kids' books, in which a sister and brother run away and sleep in the Metropolitan Museum of Art.

"Nope. Not sleeping there. It's where they blow up the balloons."

As we climb up the dingy stairway from the subway to

the street, we can hear generators humming, intermittent hissing, and the muted hustle of a crowd.

There, around the entire block that encircles the museum (a gothic Hogwartsy thing in the center), streets are closed off and clogged with them. They are round and jubilant and bouncy, and they are held down with giant nets. Men in neon-colored jumpsuits run around with hoses plugging them into different sections of balloon in the proper sequence, an arm here, a butt there, then a big red nose. Almost all the balloons are inflated: Buzz Lightyear, the Sock Monkey, a new little elf, with two or three still lying in flat, brightly colored splats on the sidewalk.

Tourist dads with their cameras around their necks and their kids up on their shoulders walk along a designated path to get a preview of the balloons. SpongeBob's banana nose sticks out from beneath a net. Snoopy's Red Baron aviator cap pushes against the ropes as if he's trying to be born.

"This is *so* cool," I tell Zoe.

"I knew you would like it," she says.

We shuffle around the block with the crowds till we get to the back side of the museum on Eighth Avenue. It's quieter over here because most of the inflation has finished. I see out of the corner of my eye that Zoe stops at Kermit the Frog.

"It's not easy being green," she mumbles, and I get a bad feeling about it. I suddenly know what the Swiss Army knife is for.

"No, Zoe, not this," I say.

"Doesn't it make you so sad to see him strapped down? His eyes are so expressive."

"They're Ping-Pong balls cut in half, Zoe. Leave him alone."

"Nope, it must be done," she says, and she tells me to be on the lookout while she begins the sawing. Security is tight, but she is wiry, wily, and dressed in black. The hissing of the helium hoses drowns out the gnawing, scratchy sound of her Swiss Army knife. When NYPD comes around the corner, I quickly unfold a balloon map that I found discarded on the path, and I ask the officer how to get to Mickey Mouse.

He has his back to Zoe, and behind him I can see she is making some headway. Kermit's webbed foot is drifting skyward toward the moon, the raw edges of the black net flopping around where he kicked himself free. She needs to act fast before anyone notices.

And work fast she does. In less than five minutes, she is back at my side, huffing and puffing. She grabs my elbow and tells me to run. We sprint up Seventy-eighth toward Central Park. If we can get to the park, we can hide. Once inside, behind a bush, we turn and look at him, Kermit-green and gangly, floating ass over elbows, swimming almost, toward the Hudson River Parkway, or some happy Sesame Street swamp in the sky.

"He's free!" Zoe exclaims. "Doesn't that make you happy?

I feel like *I'm* filled with helium." She pulls out her Polaroid and takes a photo of him wafting away. She tries to take another one, but it takes too long to crank the plastic dial and prep the next shot.

Before he's completely gone and because the moment calls for it, we sing for him, "Someday we'll find it / The rainbow connection / The lovers, the dreamers, and me . . ."

I can't say that part of me isn't enjoying this audacity business. The corners of my face hurt from smiling for so long, and my stomach muscles are tired from silently laughing. *How can you have memories if you don't have the audacity to create them?* I think. But I'm not sure audacity requires breaking the law.

"I think we just screwed a lot of people over," I say, trying to pull us back to reality.

"Who?"

"The people who made Kermit. The people who paid for him. The people who want to see him tomorrow."

"What, you think Kermit was sponsored by some mom-and-pop bodega? Macy's can afford another Kermit. And as for the people tomorrow, do you really think they'll miss one balloon? People are so overstimulated these days that they're desensitized. They can't give a shit about one issue, news story, baseball game, TV show, book, parade balloon, scandal for too long because there's another one coming down the pike to overshadow it all. We're buried in information and sensory impulses. People don't have time to care about any one thing before it's overshadowed by the next. Kermit will fill some time on the eleven o'clock news, and then he'll be forgotten. No one will care but you. Stop giving a shit!"

"I'm starving," I tell her. "Don't you need to eat?"

"The answer to that question is no, actually. But we can find you a hot dog or something."

"Great," I say.

GLUTTONY

We sleep in the penguin house at the Central Park Zoo because Zoe is good at picking locks and they don't lock it up very well. We tiptoe in. It's cold and cavernous like a damp vault. The penguins' environment is cut in half by the surface of the water, so we can watch both their land and sea behavior. They have nowhere to hide. There's about sixty of them, and they snore, standing up on the faux rocks in their tuxedos like old men at a cocktail party. Some curious chinstrap ones dive into the water. They zoom over to look at us, checking us out, making sure we can jive with their flock. Then they welcome us by slapping their wings on top of the water. They have souls, I think. It's obvious that if we have them, animals have them too.

We try to name them in order to tire ourselves out and get ready to sleep on the bed we made out of the down coats from the Long Island ladies. The underwater lamp provides the perfect night-light. "Puffy, and Stinky, and that one," I say, pointing to a seemingly selfish one who is pecking at his spouse, "that one is Ethan . . ."

Zoe ignores me.

"We should maybe talk about whether Ethan is a good penguin or a bad penguin and whether perhaps he's done some bad penguin shit that makes us want to run away from home?"

"You're trying to make things black and white, Hannah, when really it's not something you will ever understand."

"Sometimes things are black and white, Zoe. Exhibit A," I say, pointing to the flock.

"Let's just get some sleep. Big day tomorrow," she says, and she rolls over.

We stink like fish as we spend the next day at Maaco, which, in the Bronx, beneath the Cross Bronx and in the shadow of the GW Bridge, happens to be open in the wee hours of Thanksgiving morning.

We pull up next to some suspendered mafioso gentlemen in a white Oldsmobile. They probably just finished a hit and buried him, rolled in a carpet, in the woods of my hometown. It's only been two days, but I miss not waking up to the lake. I miss not seeing it sparkle outside my window. I miss my favorite birdcall in the morning. And the melted-snow fragrance of the water. I miss it with all my cells.

But Zoe is still not well. You can see it in her eyes, and I need to get her back to normal. She really is all I have in the world to depend on. I need her healthy, and I think perhaps she is right. Maybe we need to put some more distance between us and the place where she seemingly lost her mind.

So far, because of the fortuitous timing of our escape, not many people are looking for us yet. The staff of the local police department is bare bones around Thanksgiving. So probably there hasn't been much publicity around us.

But sadly, because we are white and almost middle class, it won't be long before this will hit the news. At least the local news. Maybe not *Live at Five* or anything.

So we must paint my car from its hideous opalescent turquoise, which my mom picked back in the nineties when she was a happier person, to a new, solid, inkblot black.

What they don't advertise about Maaco, but what Zoe apparently overhears from our mafia friends now smoking cigars in the already fume-filled waiting room (at least it masks the smell of fish), is that if you say the *word*, which is *tagliatelle*, then you can also buy a new set of hot license plates.

The men sit balancing the folded-up newspaper on their bellies as they look down through their reading glasses and discuss what they normally have for Thanksgiving dinner.

"My wife makes a brujol and a lasagn and some spaghett and some mozzarell." To prove you are really Italian around here, you leave the final vowels off your food.

"Don't you have any turk?" Zoe asks boldly. "Or stuff or mashed potat?"

"Ah, what do we have here? A comedienne?" the biggest one says, pointing his cigar at Zoe. The skinny gray-haired one just nods and smirks and gets back to his newspaper. He's mostly bald, the speaker, the dark black hair over his ears slicked back with some kind of old-world goo. "You're funny, kid," he says. "What'd, you get yourself in some kind of trouble in the suburbs?"

"Just a misunderstanding," Zoe says.

This makes the mafia guy laugh. "Ain't it always, kid. I ain't been nothing but misunderstood."

"I'm sure you're really a nice guy," Zoe says.

"Got three kids at home your age."

"Triplets?" she asks.

"No." He stops, frustrated with her joke. "*Around* your age. If I ever saw them hanging around the Bronx at five A.M. I'd beat them with a stick."

"Wow, that's some tough love," Zoe says, inching closer to him until her bony butt is in the seat next to his. "You're tough," she says, tracing the outline of the anchor tattoo on his hairy forearm.

This makes my skin crawl. "Zoe!" I gasp. "You'll have to excuse her, sir. She's not herself lately."

"Yeah, I may be experiencing some boundary issues," she says, looking up at him with sad eyes.

"That's what happens to you kids who are given everything," the burly man says. "You don't know when to stop."

"Yeah . . ." Zoe says. "That's not us. We get nothing handed to us. But you can believe that if you want."

Just then the Maaco guy comes into the waiting room in his jumpsuit, takes off his gas mask, and tells us our car is ready. I reach into my messenger bag for twenty rolls of quarters and start piling them into a pyramid on the counter.

"Ah, Jeezus Christ," Tony—we'll call him Tony—says. "How much is it?" He pays for our paint job and then pulls Zoe over to him by her belt loop. "Kid. Here. Take this," he says, and he sticks another two hundred-dollar bills into the waistband of her jeggings. He seems practiced at this.

"Thank you," Zoe whispers, kissing him lightly next to his ear.

Tony is confused for a second, trying to navigate the wacko energy of Zoe; then he pushes her away and says, "You're welcome," and then to me, "Watch out for her."

"I will," I say, and we are off.

"Zoeeee," I say in the parking lot. "What the hell?"

She cannot stop laughing long enough to answer me.

She starts to climb into the driver's side of our newly painted vehicle. We had to choose the cheapest paint available, and it is completely opaque and dusty like a chalkboard. It absorbs every ounce of light, completely void of color. We look criminal and suspicious in it, but we do not look like ourselves. I walk around the front of the car and look at our new New York vintage plates, the old orangey gold color from the seventies.

"We look badass," I tell Zoe.

"Bad ass. Morass. First class. Bluegrass," Zoe mumbles and then begins chewing on her fingernails to stop herself from rambling. She'd been doing this a lot. This nonsensical rhyming associating thing.

"Let me drive," I tell her. "Maybe you can nap in the passenger seat. It reclines if you twist the crank enough. It's one of the luxury features of this automobile," I joke.

The LeMans is bare bones. Half the dials on the dashboard are there for decoration. There is no AC. We cannot measure RPMs. I think it was the last American model ever made where you have to manually roll down the windows. It's a stick shift. And it's basically a box cart. It shakes when you go over seventy, and we have to lean forward when traveling uphill. But now, in its new inkblot black with its hot orange plates, it is badass. I swing it around and up a ramp to the Cross Bronx, and we *putt-putt* our way to the GW.

"Where are we headed?" I ask Zoe.

"West," she says.

"You know what's weird?"

"What?"

"I get jealous of you even when creepy old men are attracted to you. I stand there and think, *What am I? Chopped liver?*"

"You don't want to be me. You are the girl they put on a pedestal. That's where you belong. Men will always see women as either virgins or whores. It's always better to be the virgin. You don't get as much immediate action, but you get more play in the long run." Her eyes are closed beneath her aviators, so she's trying to rest, but her feet won't stop moving.

"Are you afraid of sleeping?" I ask her. "Afraid of your dreams?"

"I do have some bad ones. But no. I just don't need it anymore. Sleep. Or food. Much."

We head west on 80 as the sun rises behind us, and we slowly leave any trace of metropolis. It gets woodsier and woodsier on the sides of the highway, and the rock walls on either side of us get steeper and steeper as we approach the Delaware River. Hawks spiral above us, riding some invisible whirlpooling currents.

Once we drive over the Delaware on an ancient criss-crossed iron girder bridge, we leave all traces of city behind. We step back in time to a place where people, according to the billboards, still eat big pancake breakfasts but no longer work it off in the fields. They eat a thing here called "scrapple," which I don't think you find outside of Pennsylvania because if you haven't grown up eating a gray meaty thing called "scrapple" there is no way you would ever let it pass your lips.

We are in scrapple country, looking off in the distance at the patchwork farms and the occasional old red barn. To Zoe, in her state of mind, the landscape probably looks like a Technicolor painting by Hockney. She refuses to remove her sunglasses even though it is still overcast and windy. We pass outlet malls and tourist-trap caverns and diners that claim to be Pennsylvania Dutch. And after about two hours we see a sign for a truck stop. It is about as tall as a skyscraper, and it simply says TRUCK STOP in red and white. No one even bothered to name it.

"Land ho," Zoe suddenly calls out.

"What?" I ask.

"I've always wanted to go to a truck stop. And we could use a shower."

It's true. Every pore in my body feels like it's overflowing with gunk. My armpits feel volcanically warm and moist, and I am starting to itch. Just the suggestion of a shower makes me realize how badly I am craving one. Suddenly I would do anything for some hot water. But a truck stop?

"Are you sure? We're going to stand out," I tell Zoe.

"Standing out is my specialty when I'm in the mood for it."

"I'm more about the blending in," I say, mixing my hand in a circle.

"Just follow my lead."

A lot of truckers are working today because they get time and a half for Thanksgiving. The showers are through a door along the back wall, where scruffy-faced potbellied men in sleeveless white T-shirts wait in line holding their towels and brown leather Dopp kits.

"Two showers, please," Zoe says to the woman behind the counter. In the glass display case underneath her flabby elbow are piles of jingoistic tchotchkes, like bald eagle this and stars and stripes that. Piled in the center of the store are boxes of Pennsylvania Dutch apple pies. There are aisles and aisles filled with pork rinds and beef jerkies of all varieties. On a table in the back next to the door that leads to the diner, a taxidermist has displayed a small fox, a skunk, and a squirrel. The squirrel is on sale for seventy-five dollars.

"We don't have a ladies'," the old woman at the counter says. We know her name is Marge because we have overheard some of her conversations. She could use a shower too, by the looks of her silvery-tan hair that's pulled back in a greasy bun. Her teeth are yellow, and she plays with a red and white Bic lighter, just jonesing for her next cigarette break.

"That's okay, we'll wait," says Zoe, and I am appalled. I can only imagine one thing that is dirtier than me right now, and it is one of those shower stalls where truckers have been hocking up their mucus all morning.

"I'm all set," I tell Zoe. "There is no way I'm showering in there."

"Even if we wait until they're done?" she asks. She looks

over to the line of undershirted truckers. "And maybe buy some flip-flops. You sell flip-flops?" she asks Marge.

"Even if hell freezes over, pigs fly, and over your dead body."

"Never mind," Zoe tells the cashier. "My friend is reluctant to take advantage of your facilities. Do you at least have a ladies' bathroom?"

She points to the restrooms behind the coffee bar—some clear-glass pitchers on hot plates, bubbling with thick black liquid, and a shaker-container of nondairy creamer. "You would think with all these cows around they could get some milk," I mumble as we pass it and then duck into the bathroom.

I swab down the entire sink with wads and wads of toilet paper before I even dare to use it. We wash our faces with our loofah sponges, splash some water in our armpits, brush our teeth, change our underwear, and we are completely refreshed.

"I'm hungry," I tell Zoe. "My stomach is doing visible cartwheels. Look," I say and pull up my shirt. "And you should eat too. A nice hot open turkey sandwich for Thanksgiving. We'll use the money from your friend."

We are headed toward the door to the diner, but Zoe stops to look at the taxidermy table. "Fine," she says with a sigh, "but I'm buying that stuffed squirrel. It's on sale."

"You're kidding, right?"

"Nope. I want it, and I'm going to buy it. Today's lesson is Gluttony. Take what you want."

"You know that's another symptom of bipolar disorder. Ill-advised shopping sprees, unwise purchases."

"It's just a stuffed squirrel."

"A real stuffed squirrel for seventy-five dollars, which we need for gas. It probably has rabies."

"He's mounted on a log. And he's holding a chestnut."

"We can't afford him, Zoe."

"You can even see his real front teeth."

"I'm sorry."

"I won't take no for an answer," she says, and she brings the hideous thing with its fake plastic eyes to the cash register. Its fur is the same color as Marge's hair. Zoe tries to bargain her down, but in the end hands her one of our precious hundred-dollar bills and gets twenty-five dollars back.

In the diner she sets "Squirrely" on the table in front of the mini jukebox, and she takes a picture of it with her disposable camera. It watches us eat. I hate Squirrely, and I want to stab him with my fork.

She orders one slice of every kind of pie they have, including apple pie with melted cheddar cheese on top, takes one tiny bite of each, and then proclaims herself full, while I methodically plod through my open-faced turkey with cranberry sauce from a can, fake gravy from a jar over Wonder Bread. It actually hits the spot, and I eat the entire thing. I have no idea when we will eat again, because Zoe keeps spending our money on dead rodents.

"How much longer do you think we need to be on this adventure?" I ask her. While I was eating, she braided her hair and wrapped it around her head in a neat pillbox-shaped hair-hat.

"Um, looks like it's just beginning," she says calmly as she points to the TV, hanging from the ceiling above the counter. It has taken a break from football to show our senior pictures in split screen. In mine, I am leaning against a fake tree with a frozen look of fear on my face, while Zoe smiles naturally for the camera as she gives it the finger. Her mother cut that part out. Above our photos in orange block letters it says AMBER ALERT.

"They're looking for us," Zoe says and then pets her dead squirrel.

I try not to look at the TV, but I listen to the reporter say that we may or may not be armed with a Taser gun.

"We may?" I angrily whisper to Zoe through clenched teeth.

She lifts her hand up from beneath the table to show me she's holding an electric razor-shaped device. She smiles and whispers, "Meet Tasery."

"Zoe!" I say.

"Did you take that from Officer Franz?"

Zoe nods a little guilty child nod.

"Did you USE it on Officer Franz?"

"Of course not," she says, but she's not looking me in the eye.

"Oh jeez." I start to feel that shaky, sweaty panicky feeling you get right before you have diarrhea. "Are you serious?" I am too flustered to figure out our next move. I know truckers are finely in tune with AMBER Alerts, though, and they take them very seriously. Our first step is to sneak out of this diner.

The waitress turns her back for a second to make a vanilla shake at the counter, so Zoe and I quietly dine-and-dash. The only exit is through the gift shop, so we sneak back into Marge's domain, where she is watching the same channel and studying our photographs. Zoe slams a drinking helmet on my head as a disguise. It's a plastic hat with two beer-can-shaped holders connected to a straw on the sides. She puts a bright orange hunting cap on herself, and we dash out the door with Squirrely.

"Hurry!" Zoe says as we run across the gravel parking lot.

Adrenaline takes over, and I run fleetly without feeling my limbs. We jump into the car and, with Zoe driving, get back on Route 80, until we notice the flashing AMBER Alert signs lining the highway on both sides.

"Time for the blue roads," Zoe says. She veers off at a random exit, looks to the sky, and seems to be trying to follow an enormous black storm cloud moving westward in the wind.

BELIEF

I can't tell if Zoe is paranoid or cautious, but she keeps looking behind us, as if we're being followed.

"I feel like we saw that Honda CRV in the Bronx," she says.

"I'm sure there are a lot of Honda CRVs in the Bronx. Why do you think it's that one?"

"My dear, who's had some run-ins with the law? You or me?"

"Is it *run-ins* or *runs-in*?"

"Who's had some runs-in with the law?"

"Okay, you," I say. If you count getting caught by a cop fooling around with Jimmy Russo in the closet of the Municipal Building during her shift at Safe Ride a "run-in." Safe Ride was cancelled for good after that, in the interest of safe sex.

Zoe puts on some fingerless leather gloves and switches to high gear. "I can smell a pig from a mile away," she says.

"I don't like calling them 'pigs,'" I say. "They're heroes, actually. They are like your mom. They have to treat everyone with respect and dignity. They learn that. The good ones. The good ones are not too quick to judge people." I could see Danny as a cop one day, I think. He has the heart for it.

"Oh my god, you are so naïve. There are bad cops."

"And there are good cops."

"Well, good or bad, we have to ditch this one," she says, taking some hairpin turns through the woods at sixty miles per hour and on two wheels.

I turn around and try to find who she thinks is following us, but I don't see any headlights. "What color is the car?" I ask her.

"White," she says. "He's about a quarter mile behind us. Ask Squirrely. He knows, right, Squirrely?"

She has strapped Squirrely into the backseat with a seatbelt and adorned him with Officer Franz's aviators.

She continues driving, somehow keeping the rain cloud in her line of vision above her, while keeping an eye in the rearview. She hasn't looked straight ahead in five miles.

"Zo," I say. "Zoe, no one's back there."

"Okay," she says with a breath. "We lost them. We need to hide, though, be more careful," she says, downshifting. She turns left into a Walmart parking lot. "No one will find us here. We'll blend."

The cloud that she seems to be chasing is building on top of itself into a towering thunderhead that sits on top of Walmart like a hat.

It's three in the morning, and people are lined up around the store in pop tents in what looks like a very narrow refugee camp.

I look through the passenger window, mouth agape. "What the . . . ?"

"Welcome to Black Friday, my sweet," Zoe says.

"What are we doing here? You hate Walmart," I say.

"Well, it's a safe place to spend the night, and we should probably get some clean clothes."

I don't say a thing. I just watch the happy campers walk back and forth sharing coupons with one another.

"Go back to sleep," says Zoe. "They don't open the doors for another hour or two."

It seems like only two minutes, though, before Zoe wakes me up. I was dreaming about Danny, I think. "Come on! It's time," she says, poking me. We scramble out of the car, and Zoe drags me toward the door.

"Shouldn't we wait until the end of the line? I've heard of deaths by stampede. This many people could definitely crush us."

"No! I want to be in the thick of it."

We squish our bodies around everyone and worm our way close to the front. When I look beneath an armpit in front of me, I see a black-and-white poster taped haphazardly to the glass door entrance next to the store hours. It's our pictures! Mine and Zoe's. The split screen of photos from the AMBER Alert. It's a terrible inkblotty resolution, though. We look like one of those Rorschach psychological tests. I stick my hand beneath the arm of the guy in front of me and point to it so that Zoe sees it and then cover my mouth in surprise.

"We're famous," Zoe mouths to me.

"Notorious," I mouth back.

A blow horn sounds, and the doors open as people scream and squash themselves forward, a hungry gluttonous horde waving coupons in the air and making a wild dash for the televisions. I get smacked in the face with a flabby triceps, and Zoe catches the moment on film. I hear her winding the dial for the next shot, and I follow that sound. I can't see her. The only thing I can see are the letters *e* and *a* because my face is squashed into the Bears jersey of the gentleman in front of me.

"Zoe!" I scream.

"Allemande left," she yells. It is our secret move from the father-daughter Girl Scout square dance where we stood in for each other's fathers every year. I know she wants me to snake myself around some folks and then dart out to the left down toward the cosmetics, which most people are avoiding right now. They're all making a beeline for the electronics.

When I break free, I see Zoe grab some plaid shirts and leggings, some stiff jeans, and dry socks.

"Cool." She smiles when she sees me. "Ladies' room, pronto."

She's holding two boxes of hair dye. Honey Wheat for me and Pure Diamond for herself, a bold Marilyn Monroe platinum, which will be drastic, but it might look good with her turquoise eyes.

"We're dyeing our hair?"

"You saw the poster. If we want to be on the lam, we need disguises. It'll be fun!"

Zoe works some magic with the plaid shirts, rigging them so they fit us perfectly and hug our figures, and we change out of the sleeping-bag coats and into some new clothes. They are scratchy and cheap, but just the fact that they are clean makes them an enormous improvement.

We wet our hair in the sinks and then start squirting in the bleach. It smells like sulfur and chlorine and makes my eyes water. Zoe, because she's going from black to white, needs to leave hers in for at least an hour, so we sit on the radiator and wait. No one at Black Friday is going to risk missing out on saving their precious twenty dollars (really, that's all they could possibly be saving) by taking a bathroom break, so we have the place to ourselves.

"What's it like, anyway?" Zoe asks out of the blue. "AA."

"Well . . ." I imagine myself rubbing my hands together

in a sneaky scheming way. Maybe I can use AA to get her to "share" whatever happened at Ethan Drysdale's that night and get back to normal. Maybe I can teach her some intangibles, like serenity, acceptance, wisdom. "It's just group therapy, really. You come in, and the leader starts the Serenity Prayer. If it's a step meeting, someone starts a discussion of a step, and then people share their stories of working that step."

"What are steps?"

"They're like sequential actions you take on the road to getting sober. Step one is admitting you're powerless over your addiction. Step two is believing in God or something bigger than yourself. Step three is letting God take care of you. Step four is the hardest—taking a moral inventory of yourself. This is starting to burn," I say, wrapping my finger in some toilet paper and wiping around my hairline.

"Go rinse. So, do you believe in that stuff? That you are powerless and you need to trust God?"

We never really went to church, so AA is the closest thing I had to a religion. And secretly, I do like it. All you have to do at AA is: *Come to believe that a power greater than yourself can restore you to sanity.* That's it.

You don't have to believe that someone died and came back to life. You don't have to believe that you're God's chosen people, or that women should hide their hair, or that some guy found a golden book that told him to go west and polygamize.

You don't have to eat God's body or drink his blood. You don't even have to call him God. And you don't have to call it *him*. You call it a higher power. And you can imagine it any way you want. You can imagine your higher power as a golden pulsating egg lying on a patch of soft grass. Or you can imagine it as a supermodel. Or Scooby-Doo. Or a giant lake—my lake—into which you pour all your troubles. Your desire to drink, your hurt feelings, your sense of injustice, your unrequited loves, your epic failures, your bad hair, your big butt, your ego. You throw it all in there, maybe tie it to a rock first, and then imagine it splashing to the bottom with a satisfying *kerplunk*. You let your higher power worry about all that stuff. And then you get on with your day.

Because *this day* is all that you have.

"It makes living easier," I tell her.

"Isn't it more like giving up, though? Don't you need to take charge of your life and not surrender it to God?"

"It's the only religion I've ever known."

"Yeah, but it's for sick people, and you're not sick. Your dad is sick, right? And you need to tell yourself that every time you talk to him, so he doesn't hurt you. You need to pretend you wrote SICK across his forehead with a Sharpie, okay?"

She's right. His words sink like hooks into my flesh, and I need to make sure not to let them become who I am. But I've thought about this before, and have a hard time coming up with a single person whose forehead deserves to be labeled HEALTHY.

"Who has HEALTHY written across their forehead?" I ask her.

"I don't know," she says after a minute. "But I probably wouldn't trust them either."

"Right. Everyone's a little messed up."

I check a lock of her hair, and it's a yellowish white. "You have a little to go," I tell her.

Just then, Zoe seems to hear something and dashes for a stall.

"What?" I ask her just as she panics and sticks her head in the toilet.

"Zoe! What are you doing?"

She lifts her head out, flips it back, and wrings it out, all without making a sound. I'm guessing that's why she didn't turn on the sink, and then she sneaks to the bathroom door and holds her finger up to her lips. "Shhh," she whispers. "They're out there."

"Who?"

"The fuzz," Zoe says, and then points to a security camera that's been eyeing us this entire time.

"What do we do?" I whisper.

"Run!" she says as she bursts the door open, holding the Taser in front of her with outstretched arms like a Charlie's Angel.

I run behind her with my head down so as not to get caught in the potential cross fire or any more security cameras.

Zoe grabs a few more things from the shelves with her free hand as she runs, and then says, "Catch!" as she throws two heavy rolls of nickels to a cashier named Ryan. Then we sprint out the doors headed for the LeMans. When we get there, panting, I realize no one is chasing us.

Zoe cackles.

"Zo. What was that?"

"You should have seen your face," she laughs. "It was just a little make-believe. Wasn't it fun? Here, put some conditioner on your hair or you will be a ball of frizz." She tosses me the tube that came with the hair dye, and then dumps the rest of her booty on the hood of the car. A red slouch hat, some scissors, Cheetos, some trail mix, and mud flaps with silhouettes of silver naked girls on them.

Zoe combs out her own hair, uses the conditioner, and then begins cutting it with some barber shears she stole from cosmetics. She cuts it quickly into a cute, asymmetrical number and then dries it with a towel from the backseat. The whitish color looks great. Her bangs sweep expertly over one eye. She looks like an impish superhero.

I look in the side-view mirror of the LeMans. Honey Wheat, I have to say, does nothing for my complexion. I have reddish highlights and should have gone red. "Um, can you throw me that hat?" I ask Zoe.

"It looks great. Sort of. You can fix it when you get home," she says, primping it a little.

My hands are still shaking as I squeeze another cold glob of conditioner onto the ends of my hair. "That wasn't funny, Zoe." She knows getting busted at anything is scarier to me than almost anything else. It was a weird friendship moment where for one of the first times ever we are not on the same wavelength. "That was not funny at all."

"Oh, calm down, Hanns. Reality gets a little sad and boring sometimes. When things get like that, you have to use your imagination. A little make-believe goes a long way. People forget that as they get old. The power of pretending."

"Um. Yeah," I tell her, using my own power of pretending to convince myself that wasn't a little weird. "But you scared me. Let me in on the joke next time," I tell her. "We're in this together. "

"Okay, Hannah Banana," she says, grabbing me around the shoulders. "I'm sorry."

GOD

While Zoe is pimping our vehicle with the mud flaps, I notice that Squirrely is gone. His log sits empty and abandoned in the hatchback, and his chestnut has rolled all the way into the back corner of the car.

"Where's Squirrely?" I ask Zoe as we climb into the car.

"I set him free while you were asleep."

"Where?"

"I just pulled up to some woods, put his log down on the ground, and let him hop away."

"Zoe, he has no organs," I say.

"Well, he didn't need them. Hurry up, there's a tornado watch near Toledo." Zoe had apparently gotten a five-finger discount on an old transistor radio that reported the weather in a robot voice transmitted by local weather stations. It made scratchy static sounds as she turned the dial and held it up close to her ear. My dad always had one in the kitchen. He called it Charlie and found it more reliable than all the fancy Doppler radar computers at the TV station. He always listened to Charlie before he headed out to work.

"So we're storm chasing now?"

"Unless you have something you want to see."

"I would like to see you fall asleep. I'll drive. You sleep," I say, and I wonder what I would like to see on this trip. Maybe Mount Rushmore. Chicago? The Mall of America? The Grand Canyon?

School doesn't teach geography or U.S. history anymore, so I learned most of it from American Girl doll catalogs. We could never afford to get an actual doll, but Zoe and I read the catalogs and the books from the library, and we would categorize the rich girls we met according to which doll we thought they might have. She's a Molly. That one's Samantha. The true iconoclasts had Kaya dolls, which is the one we both coveted the most. She came with a pet wolf.

What I really want to see right now is Danny Spinelli. I try to push that out of my mind. How I wanted to be absorbed into his body. And I think that's probably not healthy.

"Is it healthy to want to be absorbed into his body?"

"That's what an orgasm feels like."

"WHAT?"

"Well, for a split second before it happens there's this sense of nothingness. Like you and he have melded and become just light. Just energy. You become Nothing for a split second. Or maybe you die or become God. Because when everything comes rushing back, like a prolonged luxurious sneeze throughout your entire body, that's what you say."

"What?"

"Oh my god. That's what most people say anyway. So maybe God is orgasm."

"You could probably get arrested for saying that in this part of the country."

"Churchy people know that. Why do you think they have so many kids? You're the only one who doesn't know that. Yet, anyway. Have you ever?"

"What?"

"Met God."

"I don't think so."

"You would know if you did."

"Then, no."

"I want to make sure that you've got that in place before I go."

"Where are you going?"

"Nowhere," Zoe says distantly and then leans her head against the window looking toward the sky.

I take some woodsy roads through the flat subdivisions of Ohio. There's only one thing I am extremely confident about, and that is my sense of direction. I can just feel where on the map I am and sense where on the map I want to go. I attribute it to my Lenni Lenape ancestors. I keep driving toward where I remember the sun setting and then making occasional rights to get us to the north.

I reach over and turn down the weather radio, which, despite its mechanical over-enunciated monotone, seems to get excited when it talks about the tornado.

"A toRnAdo is expeCted in LUcas county between sev-en A.M. and sev-en ThirTy."

Its robot voice reminds me of Noah, but I do not bring up his name yet. He is my ace in the hole. The thing I mention when I know we really need to turn around. One allusion to Noah, and I know Zoe will be ready to head for home.

Zoe closes her eyes and rests her head on the headrest.

Finally, I think. She is finally going to rest and get back to herself. I could sense some of her old self returning in our last conversation. She was speaking without feeling rushed by the hurried landslide of her thoughts. Her brain gets like that *I Love Lucy* episode where Lucy's working in the chocolate factory and the conveyor belt gets ahead of her and the chocolates keep coming and coming and there's nothing you can do but start swallowing them.

And now that she is quiet for a moment, I try to think for myself. Part of me knows we need to get back and fess up. Face the music. Apologize to Officer Franz. Atone for our sins. Move on. But I don't want to do that until I know Zoe can make a case for herself. She needs to be calm and reasonable or this whole trip will have been for naught. They'll just put her right back in the slammer. I'll see how she seems when she wakes up, and then I'll suggest turning around.

"I'm not asleep."

"What?"

"You just said, 'I'll see how she seems when she wakes up,' and I'm not asleep."

"I didn't *say* that out loud, Zoe. I was thinking it."

"No, you said it."

"No, Zoe. I swear I didn't." I am looking in her eyes, instead of the winding road, when I feel a terrible thump beneath the steering wheel and then beneath the back wheels.

"What was that?" I ask.

"I don't know," Zoe says. "Pull over."

I ease the LeMans over to the side of the road and get out. In the middle of the yellow center line lies a throw-pillow-sized lump of black fur.

"Oh my god, I hit that!" I say sadly. "What is it?"

Zoe walks to the center of the road, and I look both ways before following her. She squats down and reaches toward it, a raccoon. His pointy snout points to the south.

"Don't touch it, Zoe," I say. "It could be sick." But it's too late. She strokes her hand down its coarse wild animal fur. And then she cries a little. A single tear. Which is rare. I very rarely see her cry. And I'm surprised it's over a dead raccoon.

"Really, you're crying about this," I start to say, when the square of fur starts to shake back and forth a little. There is a soft clicking, purring sound. Zoe puts a hand on either side of the animal and bends down to listen for a heartbeat. Then she lifts it and stands it upright. The raccoon opens its eyes, finds its footing, and waddles creepily back into the woods.

"It was just stunned," Zoe says, a little spacey, as if the whole experience took something out of her.

"Um, what just happened?" I ask her.

"I told you. I have newfound abilities," she says in an eerie monotone.

"Two words for you: hand sanitizer," I say.

When we get back to the car, I squirt copious amounts of it into her hands, and she sits back down and stares straight ahead.

The wind is beginning to pick up. A gust of it almost knocks us off the shoulder and into the ditch that leads to a little creek below us.

"Tornado, please," Zoe requests. And I continue heading northwest. My father is a weatherman, which is different from being a meteorologist, so I don't know much, but I do know that tornadoes usually happen in the spring, not the fall, and they like big wide-open spaces. Like Kansas. Ohio is mostly flat, but we're in a slightly hilly part of it, and I seek lower ground in order to find a flat place with a break in the trees.

Both the sunrise and the wind are behind us now. The wind almost lifts our tiny car off the ground as we speed along a flat two-lane highway. Everyone else, it seems, is heeding the tornado warning and staying off the road.

Above us, the heavens collect in a dense city of

condensation. Clouds are building on top of one another. Some of them seem to be dipping to the ground, opening up their bottoms toward the earth like steam shovels. The wind starts to blow one of them into a black spiral about the diameter of a football stadium, and it starts to sink and spin, whipping haphazardly toward the ground.

"I need to be there!" Zoe points. "Where it's touching."

"We can't be there. We are here, which is amazing enough. Take a picture."

Bright flashes of light crackle inside the storm because it has collected and snapped up power grids. Natural lightning starts to zap around it.

"Closer!" Zoe begs at the edge of her seat. She snaps a picture through the windshield and turns the cranky dial to get ready for another shot.

I take a left and drive toward the storm. But the wind is so strong I can barely accelerate.

"Let's get out," Zoe says when we get to where she thinks it's close enough. "Here, you should wear a helmet," she says and she plonks the drinking helmet from the truck stop onto my head. She dons the bright orange hunting cap with the earflaps, and we both get out the passenger side and stay between the car and the open door.

The spiral is headed straight for us. But at the last minute it takes a hard right. It sounds like a seventeen-car pileup. Screeching and wailing and whistling. A roaring freight train.

Hail the size of softballs starts to thud into the wet earth around us. I pick up a piece and show it to Zoe, incredulous. The storm moves to the east, slapping against our down coats, whipping our hair against our faces, slamming us against the car. My drinking helmet flies up and away to the land of Oz. We hold each other down. My ears pop. I can't hear a thing, but I can feel Zoe lifting toward the sky.

I grab her ankle and use all of my strength to pull her back to the ground, and then I lie on top of her in a starfish formation until everything is suddenly quiet.

For three full minutes we hear nothing. There is nothingness.

Then a bird starts to chirp, checking if the coast is clear, a car drives by, and the sun picks itself up above a flat purple cloud.

"Oh my god!" Zoe shouts. "That was exactly like sex. Well, the reverse order. The rushing and roaring came first and then the nothingness and then the gentle awakening. But you get the idea. Now you have met God."

"I thought it would be better than that," I mumble.

I am still lying on top of her because I can't connect the messages in my brain to the muscles that are supposed to move my limbs. "You need to let me go," Zoe says. "You are holding on to me."

"Dude. So you wouldn't blow away."

"When you are ready, you will let me go," she says dreamily and looks again to the sky.

KARMA

We drive northwest for an hour to Michigan. Michigan is much like rural New Jersey, except it's flattened out and well planned and pristine. Michigan would *be* New Jersey if you ran over it with a steamroller, excavated everything, and then put it back in neat rows with lots of space for everyone to move around in. It is practical and pretty, and it's a place where nothing spontaneous happens. This is a place where nothing happens unless people sit around and have a meeting about it first. The people are mostly white, which is weird, and the squirrels are sometimes black, also weird.

To distract ourselves, I am trying to find the license plates of all fifty states, while Zoe gets enraged by bumper stickers. We follow a truck whose bumper reads GUN CONTROL MEANS BEING ABLE TO HIT YOUR TARGET. Zoe is driving behind him, tailgating, her fury building.

Finally she pulls to his left and makes me duck. She asks me to roll down my window and motions for the other driver to do the same. She screams out the window at him, "Are you part of a well-regulated militia?"

"What?" the guy says. He's fat and balding and has prickly short gray hair growing from all parts of his body.

"Leave him alone," I insist from the seat well I was ordered to crouch into.

The guy, incredibly, thinks Zoe is coming on to him. He smirks and winks his fat eyelid. She screams at him again. "Hey, asshole, I said, ARE YOU PART OF A WELL-REGULATED MILITIA?"

He just holds up his hands because he can't hear her.

Zoe continues racing to stay at his side and then holds up Tasery and aims it toward him through the window. "You," she says. "You are my target!" and then she pulls the trigger, and a tiny bolt of lightning zaps between the rods at the end of the Taser. The bald man gets on his cell phone. He's too wrapped up in being a man's man to take her seriously, so he laughs, dismissing her, which infuriates Zoe even more. She hates to be dismissed.

"Roll up the window," Zoe says to me. And then she somehow coaxes ninety mph out of the poor LeMans to pull ahead and away.

"Um. That was quite a display," I say, trying to unfurl myself from under-the-seat asana.

She's still riled up and red faced with rage.

"Take a breath," I tell her. "Wild guess, but this might be the kind of outburst that people mistake for mental illness," I try.

"Mental illness? I'm expressing myself. What do you want me to do, write a well-crafted letter to the editor? That's not me. I'm a guerrilla fighting for what I believe in on the highways of America. I'm Neal Cassady, and you're Sal Paradise. And you love me. I am your muse," she says, taking her eyes off the road to look at me.

"The only people for you 'are the mad ones, the ones who are mad to talk, mad to be saved, desirous of everything at the same time, the ones who never yawn or say a commonplace thing, but burn, burn, burn like fabulous yellow Roman candles exploding like spiders across the stars,'" she quotes from *On the Road*. "You're living through me, Hannah Banana. I need to teach you how to live on your own. And burn like a Roman candle." She leans forward and looks to the sky. "And there's not much time." A pinkish, iridescent cloud that looks like the inside of an enormous oyster shell whirlpools above us and seems to follow us like the moon. "They're getting closer. I can hear the frequency of them. It's like static on the radio, but more organized and symphonic. I think they're inside that cloud. And they're waiting for me to ditch you, probably. But I have some more to teach you. Do you ever see their shadows? In your peripheral vision? They move around us all the time. And they know our names, too. Sometimes they whisper my name in my ear to wake me in the morning. Do you ever hear them?"

"Um. No," I venture, starting to freak out. When she's

talked about "them" before, they always sounded innocent, like imaginary friends. This latest report sounds so clinical. Less like a fantasy and more like a "symptom." A scary adult disease. "So where are we headed?" I ask, exhaling.

"I have a cousin in Ann Arbor," she says, keeping an eye on the cloud in the rearview.

"Does your cousin have a bathtub?" I ask.

"Let's hope so."

"Zoe, you're a smart person."

"Yes."

"So you know we're on the run because something happened to change your mood. There was a trigger. A stimulus. And then a response."

"That sounds very logical, Hannah, but there are parts of this you don't understand. There are different systems of logic that exist in dimensions you can't see."

"Nothing happened with Ethan, then?"

Zoe looks at me for a second, disappointed. She shakes her head, says nothing, and continues driving, still preoccupied with the cloud that's now directly in front of us.

As promised, Ann Arbor is arboreal. The eponymous trees are neat and beautiful and fit into the plan. They are tame and innocuous and often stand happily alone. So unlike the tangled mess of trees in the Jersey woods I'm used to. In Jersey, you can't see the light for them. The trees. The tangled deep mess of everything can choke you in New Jersey.

These trees have room to breathe and grow and become happy independent thinkers. I am suddenly jealous of them.

"I'm jealous of the trees."

"I'm angry at the bees," Zoe says, laughing. "What are you talking about?"

"Nothing."

Cousin Jimmy lives on campus at the University of Michigan in an apartment above a lazy, dingy, loungy hippie café with mismatched chairs and velvety brass and copper-colored couches from the twenties. It's called Muffin Top in homage to the college girls who wear their jeans slung too low across their pillowy, beer-fed hips.

We have to walk through the café kitchen and into its broom closet that smells like moldy mop to get to Jimmy's staircase. He's in a wide-open red plaid robe and light blue boxer shorts when he opens the door for us. He is slender and beautiful, and his shiny, slack, black hair hangs in front of one eye. The other eye takes us in.

"Cuz," he says. He is completely unperturbed. I don't think anything could "plus" him at all. He lets us in and then walks himself back to bed—a mattress on the floor in the room at the end of the hall.

According to Zoe, he couldn't afford to come home for Thanksgiving so he took a job caring for the mice in the science labs for four days. Aside from him, and some students from faraway places like Saudi Arabia or something, the campus is empty.

"I didn't know you had a cousin," I say to Zoe.

"I do."

"A hot cousin."

"Since he's, like, my cousin, I don't notice his hotness. You think he's hot?"

"Smoking," I say.

"You should definitely leave the *g* off when you say that," Zoe says, cringing.

The apartment is empty except for a scratchy plaid couch and a coffee table made out of a couple of suitcases piled on top of one another. There is a TV on top of a milk crate, and that's about it.

Luckily there is a bathtub, and I have never in my life been so happy to see one. It's a college bathtub, though, and it hasn't been cleaned since Jimmy moved in, so there is brown grime around the edges. I try not to think about it as I turn up the hot water and stand in the shower for ten minutes before even reaching for the soap. I wash my hair with my special shampoo, and then Zoe throws a tube of conditioner at me. "You must use that. Your hair is already the color of straw."

Zoe washes her face in the sink and brushes her teeth with my toothbrush, which, because it is Zoe, does not bother me as much as you think it would.

She preens a little in the mirror. She is the kind of person who never looks bad. Even with platinum hair that she cut by herself at Walmart, even after getting hit by a tornado, she looks beautiful. I am the kind of person who has some really good days and some really bad days in the looks department. I have an erratic kind of beauty. I didn't even glance at myself before climbing into the shower, in the hopes that when I'm at least clean, I can do something to avoid looking like a scarecrow in my new straw-colored hair and flannel shirt.

When I get out, Zoe steps gracefully into the shower and uses the same towel I used, so as not to be an imposition. She gets dressed and then finds a blow dryer and a round brush and gets to work making me look a little cuter than I did when I got here. She puts some makeup on my eyes to make them pop and tries a little bronzer to change the color of my wan complexion.

"Cute, but you should still wear the hat," she says.

"What are we getting ready for?"

"I don't know, but it's good to be ready."

Zoe sits open legged on cousin Jimmy's dirty living room floor and pulls out her atlas. She turns on the Weather Channel and starts using a sharp compass-type instrument to measure out some kind of angles and vectors on the maps.

I try to nap on the scratchy couch but I can't stop thinking about things. Like the entire biosphere of microorganisms that must be living between the cushions.

"What are you doing?" I say.

"Figuring out how much time I have," she says without looking up. The symbols she's writing on the map are foreign. Not the Greek of calculus. Swirls and squiggles. Weird sharp angles. Pentagons. It's pentagonal, this language. Nothing I've ever seen.

"What's with the pentagons?"

"Five is special to them. Like four is to us. Probably because they experience an extra dimension."

Jimmy shuffles out of his room, opens the refrigerator, grabs a jug of orange juice, and guzzles deeply with his whole body as if he is swimming in it. Then he wipes his mouth and goes back to bed.

"You still think he's hot?" Zoe asks.

"Uh-huh," I say, and I sneak away down the hall, looking for a landline.

I'm feeling a little in over my head in the middle of the country with Zoe seemingly losing her mind. More talk of "them," studying the weather, the ancient hieroglyphics she's drawing on the map. I just need to make a connection with home. Talk to one person so I'm not so alone in this.

I actually am starting to miss my mom, believe it or not, but instead I dial Danny, whose number I have committed to memory.

"Hello," he says. "Michigan? Hannah, is that you?"

I'm so relieved to hear his voice I almost cry. I'm about to say, "Danny?" when I hear her again. Rebecca. "Who is it?" she whines. And I hang up immediately. I don't know why I was trying the same thing and expecting different results. I think that's the actual definition of a fool.

Zoe is still watching the Weather Channel when I get back to the living room.

The Weather Channel should make me think of my father, but the best thing about this trip is that it's helped me stop thinking about him. Not thinking about him for the first time in my life has been liberating. For the first time in my life, I'm not worried about whether he's lonely, or eating right, or alive, basically, and not spiraling into a depression that will lead to his suicide.

I suddenly realize this: Never really knowing what to expect from the person who's in charge of you—who might at any minute lose control, or beg you for forgiveness, or insult you, or kill himself, or accidentally drive off a cliff—takes a lot out of a person.

Walking on eggshells, so as not to provoke this person's fiery raging outbursts, is exhausting. It is like this old seventies kids' show I found on TV Land once where a family accidentally traveled back into prehistoric times and couldn't get back to the present. They had to live in a cave and worry constantly about getting attacked by the Tyrannosaurus rex. Stuff like that can mess up your fight-or-flight response and leave it stuck forever in overdrive.

It's been nice to let all that go. And I obviously have nothing to get back to in the Danny department.

I breathe and sink into cousin Jimmy's dirty couch. I let myself fall asleep, and I dream about storms clearing, some grass growing, and me standing on my knees building a white picket fence around a square of it. Inside the square, a tree grows by itself.

When I wake Jimmy is dressed.

He's got Zoe's skinny legs and her fashion sense. In fact, he might be wearing Zoe's clothes. Tight black jeans, combat boots, a black T-shirt, and a cropped plaid swing shirt.

He and Zoe are sitting on the floor drinking tea.

"You ready, sleepyhead?" Zoe asks.

"For what?"

"We're going to feed the rats."

The rats live in the basement of the science building. It is concrete and bunkerish and plunged deep into the earth. We scramble across campus into the bunker and down the stairs and find the walls and walls of cages across from the laboratories.

Jimmy puts on a medical mask while he cranks the stereo. And he gets to work.

"We're not going to find any weird mutated rats, are we? Like ones with human ears growing on their backs?" I saw a picture of that in *National Geographic* once, and I couldn't burn it from my memory. "They don't have, like, ebola or anything, do they?"

"No. This is very basic research. Cancer research, mostly,"

Zoe says. Since his one-word greeting, I have yet to hear Jimmy's voice. He's shy. Another of my favorite qualities in a boy.

He goes about his business, grabbing the food and cage shavings from a supply closet. He works to the rhythm of the music without seeming too dancey—he pulls open the bottoms of the cages, and shakes them into a rolling garbage can. Then he refills the cages with fresh paper.

"These aren't rats," I say. "They're mice."

"Same thing," says Zoe.

"No. These guys are cute," I say. "Can I hold one?"

"Control group," Jimmy says without looking up, and he points to a row of cages with red tags hanging off them. These are the normal mice who haven't been force-fed obscene quantities of Splenda.

I reach in and let a brown one crawl onto my hand. He stands up on two feet, looks me in the eye, and blinks a couple of times. I use the pad of my index finger to pet him on his soft head, and then I lower my hand to the floor so he can run away. He looks at me for a second, unsure of himself. "Go! Be free," I whisper insistently.

This makes Zoe look up from the microscope she was peering into. "Hey. Pied Piper. What are you doing?"

"Nothing," I say. "It's just one. It's not his fault we get cancer. He doesn't deserve this."

"You're right. It's not their fault. Let's do another one."

Zoe reaches into the cage and grabs a white mouse with red eyes. "Aw. She's pretty."

"Right?"

"Go, little lady." Zoe puts her down, and she skitters across the sterile tile to a hole around the radiator and disappears.

Jimmy is too distracted by the music and the cages on the other side of the room to realize what we're doing.

"One more?" I ask, giggling. I hadn't laughed in a while. Days, it seemed. Weeks? So my laugh inspires a smile to work its way across Zoe's face.

The laugh breaks a seal and unleashes a passionate fury of emancipation. We open cage after cage and hold each mouse first, acknowledging their tiny noses and whiskers and tiny little claws that tickled across our hands. With each freed mouse a tiny mouse-sized weight lifts from my chest. We release about a dozen mice, and Zoe starts singing, before Jimmy finally turns around.

"Dudes, *what* are you doing?" he says, while Zoe slowly finishes her verse and then looks up at him with a sheepish grin. He watches a mouse scurry in a zigzag formation and run between his feet before heading for a radiator pipe and disappearing into the floor. "Do you know how hard it is to get these work-study jobs?"

Zoe and I put our heads down in shame.

"Sorry," I mumble.

"This is *science*," Jimmy says. His voice cracks a little. He really believes in science, the way some people believe in the Constitution, or the Bible, or the Chicago Bears.

"No," I say, suddenly finding my voice. "This is mousicide. And for what? To confirm that people should eat food? If everyone just ate *food* and not corn syrup and guar gum and carrageenan and Splenda, we wouldn't even get cancer. No one gets cancer in Sweden."

"Says the girl who sells hot dogs," Zoe says.

"My hot dogs are all-natural."

Zoe triumphantly holds out a mouse. "He deserves a better life!" Then she puts him down onto the floor.

"That's the last one. Stop," Jimmy says through his mask. His hands fall to his sides; his shoulders slump a little as he stares at us with the visible eye.

"Okay," we say, giggling. "Sorry."

We help him then, so he can finish faster and give us a tour of the campus. We do some window-shopping around the outskirts and then turn in to the grassy, tree-filled area of the center of campus called the Diag.

The campus is like a palace. The buildings are gray and Gothic and beautiful. The ground is flat, so flat that I can distinguish a slight curve to the Earth as if we're taking big steps on top of the world. I can't believe someone built this place for the sole purpose of advancing the minds of young people. Sometimes it seems like no one cares about that anymore. It's holy.

We sit in a tree in the middle of the Diag and just watch how the setting sun changes the color of the glass and heavy stone bricks from gray to yellow and pink and purple.

"Do you believe in God?" I ask Jimmy.

"I believe that everything happens for a reason. Is that believing in God?"

"You are lucky to be able to come here," I say.

"You will end up someplace like this too," he says.

"How do you know?"

"Because you deserve it," he says, swinging his boots back and forth. "It's the law of karma. You do everything right, and good things will come your way. It's science. Equilibrium. Homeostasis."

"How do you know I do everything right?" I ask.

"She does," Zoe pipes up, swinging down from a higher branch and hanging from her knees. Her silver hair hangs straight down in front of us like tinsel.

"You deserve it," Jimmy says again. His one exposed eye shyly looks up and finds one of mine.

And for some reason that comment is painful to me. It cuts into me like a knife and brings tears to my eyes. "Everything happens for a reason," I mumble. And that was my reason for knowing him. To think I might deserve things.

I might deserve science labs and titrating pipettes and a dorm room and libraries and professors and the time to figure things out.

I also apparently deserve to kiss Jimmy, because when we get back to his apartment, Zoe disappears on purpose to allow this to happen. We sit up on the edge of his mattress on the floor, neither of us comfortable enough to lie down with the other. And it's nice, the kissing. If only to provide me with a baseline of hotness with which to compare my kissing with Danny. With Danny, it's explosive and immediate and intense. This kissing was just comfortable and tepid and something to do to fill the time. We decide to talk instead, holding hands, looping our fingers around each other's but not letting them stray beneath any garments. And he listens. He finally asks me what we're doing on the road, and I tell him about Zoe "needing some space."

"Do you think she's okay?" I ask him, before we finally lie down to fall asleep, "or do you think we should go home and get her help?"

"Zoe always lands on her feet," he says. "She's a cool cat. Don't worry about Zoe."

Easy for him to say. He doesn't have to endure her sticking her wet finger in his ear at six in the morning I open my eyes and turn my head. Her eyes are six inches away from me on my pillow. They are bright and mad and urgent.

"Time to go," she says.

KNOWING WHAT YOU WANT
(THERE IS PROBABLY A FRENCH WORD FOR IT)

We lose a day on the road. Just hauling across Illinois and Iowa. Spinning wheels. "There's no reason to stop here," Zoe says, leaning forward against the steering wheel as if this will make the car go faster. She's obsessively hitting the scan button trying to find a tolerable song on the radio. We haven't heard about the AMBER Alert since Ohio, and I think maybe people have forgotten about us.

I collect thirty-eight states on my license plate list, which does not really impress her at all. I even got Hawaii.

"Where are we going?" I ask.

"Where do you want to go?"

"I don't know." It's the Saturday after Thanksgiving. I was going to suggest perhaps we head for home. Part of me is holding out a tiny bit of hope that we can be home on

Monday for school. But that would mean we'd have to turn around today. And it would mean facing Danny, and I don't know if I'm ready for that. "Home?" I venture.

"Home on the range?" she asks. "Where the buffalo roam? Where the deer and the antelope play?" Zoe says hopefully. "Whereseldomisheardadiscouragingword?" she sneaks in before I can interrupt.

"Home as in New Jersey," I say. "Home, home on the lake."

"Not yet," she says, getting serious. "Come on. We have the whole frontier laid out in front of us. It's manifest destiny. We can go wherever we want. You just need to know what you want. You can't *get* what you want until you know what it is. That's your next lesson. You need to know what you want."

"Is there a word for that?"

"Um, there's probably a French word for it. We'll start simply. Do you like chocolate or vanilla?"

"I don't know."

"Cats or dogs?"

"Both."

"What's your favorite band?"

"I just like music."

"Hannah. Seriously. You need to form some opinions. Where do you want to go? In the entire United States?"

"I really don't know," I say. I've only had time to respond

to things. My job has been putting out fires. Not steering my fate. I take a deep breath and close my eyes and try to visualize something. *I deserve this*, I think. All I see at first are the lane lines of the highway bombarding me like bullets to the center of my forehead. Then I see the oily slick of black tar far on the horizon that disappears as we get close to it. Then when I finally relax, I see fur. White shaggy beardy fur with the light of the sun behind it. A face slowly materializes in the middle of it. It's a buffalo. But it's white.

"Fine. It would be interesting to see a buffalo," I say. "Roaming. Not in captivity." The ones in the cave paintings, I think. The ones the Plains Indians killed with spears. It would feel like we stepped back in time to see a buffalo.

The sky gets bigger as, by evening, we head west across South Dakota. There is corn, corn, and more corn at first. And there is that sky. It feels as if we can drive right up into it. We are now entirely at its mercy. Entirely overexposed in our tiny black bug of a car.

I look in some brochures we took from a rest stop, and notice that we're blowing past all the good things to see: the Corn Palace, Wall Drug, Mount Rushmore, the Badlands. We're just trying to get to Wyoming, where we believe we might spot some buffalo.

"You don't want to see the Laura Ingalls Wilder Homestead?" Zoe asks when she sees it advertised on a road sign.

"No interest."

"That's blasphemous. An affront to girlhood. Un-American."

"You did *not* read those books."

"Uh-huh."

"No you didn't. I tried to read book one, and there were seven chapters about building the front door."

"They get better. You sure? No Laura Ingallsy . . . ? Please."

"Nope. I know what I want."

"Fair enough."

We do stop at one touristy place called Indian City, because Zoe loves places called "city" even more than she loves places called "world." She wanted me to name my hot dog cart Hot Dog City, but it didn't make the cut.

Indian City is terribly depressing. It is at the edge of the rez, and they sell some cheap turquoise jewelry and some blankets along with some Indian City bumper stickers, which Zoe buys, and other random plastic crap like mini drums, plastic pinto horses, and rubbery toy tomahawks. They have also forced some woman dressed in traditional garb to sit in the window, as if she were in a diorama at a museum, so you can watch her make a beaded purse.

"We should free her," Zoe says.

"Maybe she wants to be here. This is her job. She's not being held here against her will."

"We can at least buy her dinner."

Zoe approaches the woman, who is in a bad mood,

probably from having to be ogled by tourists as if she were an animal in a cage. "Hello," Zoe says. "My friend and I would like to buy you some dinner. Do you get a dinner break?"

The woman ignores her and keeps stringing beads onto her needle. She has long gray braids with a feather braided into a small piece in the front.

"Do you use a fish-bone needle or what?" Zoe asks.

"Take a look around, Einstein," the woman finally says, adjusting the blanket she has over one shoulder. "Where would I find a fish?"

"There must be a river or something. The great Nebraska river."

"That what they teach in those big-city schools?"

Zoe inspects the woman's design.

"Wow, it's more floral and intricate than I would have imagined. I thought it would be more geometrical."

"Because we're primitive?"

"No," Zoe says, looking over the old woman's shoulder. "Oh. I see. You use two needles. Cool." Zoe is fascinated with the design and the needlework. "You could also do it like this," she says, and she takes the woman's purse and does some kind of nimble manipulation with the waxed thread that is textured to mimic the buffalo sinew that they used to use.

The woman is shocked for a second but then captivated by what Zoe has done to her design. She takes it back and tests it dubiously, pulling at the beads to see if Zoe's method actually secured them, and then nods.

"I have an appreciation for the needle arts."

"I see that," the woman says, standing up. "My name is Rosemarie."

"What's your Indian name?" Zoe asks her.

"We stopped doing that in, like, 1864. We buy our clothes at the mall and work stupid desk jobs, just like you, Einstein."

"But if you did have one. What would it be?"

"My father called me Little Cornflower."

The design on the little pouch was, in fact, a cornflower, expertly created in a purplish slate blue.

"You kind of outgrew that, though. And Big Cornflower just doesn't sound good."

"Right."

"I'll just call you Rosemarie."

"Which is my name."

"Rosemarie, can we buy you a hot dog?"

Indian City sells hot dogs warmed over on one of those roller things they use at 7-Eleven. The hot dogs are shiny with grease, smoky-smelling, and red, and they are severely, incredibly processed with things a body doesn't recognize as food. You could tell by the smell of them.

"I don't eat those things."

"Good for you," I tell her.

"Come in the back. I'll make you some fry bread."

"The back" is what you would expect it to be. A soulless

room behind the Employees Only door that houses a card table, a coffee machine, and a hot plate next to a rusty old sink. Crass graffiti is Sharpied to the back of the door in an intricate overlapping pattern like lace.

Fry bread is like funnel cake from Pennsylvania but without sugar. Rosemarie drops some dough into a skillet filled with oil and sizzles us up a snack. She explains that Native Americans developed fry bread when they were given handouts of white flour and shortening by the government and then told to start walking across the country to some new wasteland reservation with designated boundaries. It was easy to make and carry with them when they were forced from where they were to wherever the government wanted them to end up.

"So it's like matzo," I say.

"Now, this one here is a genius, Einstein." Rosemarie points at me. "You should stick with her. Yes. It's like Native American matzo, except we were being forced into captivity, not fleeing from it like the Jews from Egypt. But we, too, eat it as a symbol of our survival."

"But it's disgusting."

"Not when you get used to it," she says. She stretches her bubbly skillet-shaped piece of bread until a piece rips off and she folds it into her mouth.

"Hey, Rosemarie. My friend and I were discussing something. Do you know what you want?"

"Fry bread," she says, licking some grease off her fingers.

"No. Do you know what you want out of life? Is it well defined?"

"I used to want a man."

"A specific man?"

"Yes."

"What happened?"

"I got him."

"Oh," Zoe says.

"Yeah. *Oh.* You need to be careful when you get what you want. My advice is to lower your expectations."

"See," I tell Zoe.

"See, nothing. The trick is to want more than just a man, right, Rosemarie?"

"I don't know. Maybe the trick is not to want."

But that doesn't seem right even to me. It will give me something to think about, though, as we finish driving across this enormous state just to get to a buffalo.

SAYING YES

Rosemarie gives Zoe a couple of ancient buffalo-bone needles, some leather, and some beads to take with her and practice her own designs. She shows her how to pop the needle only halfway through the leather so that the stitches remain invisible. They hug, and I think about what we can give her in return. All we have are rolls of coins, a weather radio, a red slouchy hat, my copy of *The Brothers Lionheart.*

I place the slouch hat on the back of her head, and with her long braids, it looks really good. Zoe snaps a picture of her, and we're about to get back on the road.

Rosemarie looks at me then. She stares me in the eye. The greenish edge of her iris has weakened and slackened with age, and it seems to leak into the white of her eye. Still, she looks at me intensely until I have to look away.

"What is it?" I ask.

"Nothing," she says, shaking her head. "I just thought maybe you knew something. But that's impossible."

"Knew what?"

"Never mind."

"What?"

"I just had a flash about the white buffalo when I looked in your eyes."

"What is the significance of a white buffalo? Hypothetically, if I had seen one or something."

"The white buffalo is our Jesus. The hope of all nations. White Buffalo came to us in the form of a woman and taught us to pray, and then she turned back into a calf, left, and promised to come again to unite all the people of the Earth. The black, the red, the yellow, and the white," she says as she points to the four colors of a cheap feathered Indian headdress stapled to the wall. "All the races of man."

"I may have seen one. Randomly. In, like, a vision as I was staring at the highway."

Rosemarie looks at me again. "You a white girl?"

"Mostly," I say.

"What's the other part?"

"Maybe Delaware, but from a long time ago when they were, like, still in New Jersey."

"The white buffalo came to you. You should smoke a peace pipe."

"No. I don't smoke," I say.

"Dude. A Lakota woman asks you to smoke a pipe to honor the white buffalo and save the planet, you do not decline," Zoe says without looking up from the toy tom-tom she's been beating in an annoying way for the past ten minutes. She's jittery again and rifling distractedly through the bins of Indian City schlock.

"It's okay," Rosemarie says, putting up her hands like a Jewish grandmother. "The girl doesn't want to smoke, she doesn't have to smoke."

"I know about reverse psychology."

"Hannah. It's a peace pipe. It's not heroin."

"I know about peer pressure."

"It's okay," Rosemarie says again.

"No. It's not okay," Zoe says. "Hannah, you need to say yes . . . If you say yes to life, you can find exhilaration and ecstasy."

"You can also find devastation and disappointment," I say. "And lung cancer."

"You're going to find those anyway," Zoe says. "But you can't get to ecstasy without saying yes."

"She's right about that," Rosemarie says, coughing, practically hacking up a lung.

"Oh my god. *Fine.*"

It was hanging by a leather strap on the back of the dirty rusty unisex bathroom door in Indian City. It looked like a hollow stick adorned in the middle with a short sleeve of beads. At the end was affixed a bone of some sort. Or an antler that was hollowed out into a cylinder.

Two white feathers hung off the side, along with some ratty leather fringe.

Rosemarie takes it off the hook and puts the seat down on the toilet before sitting down on it. She pulls some plant matter from her beaded pouch and packs the cylinder with it. Then she lights the pipe with a novelty lighter shaped like Sitting Bull that has the $1.99 Indian City price tag still stuck to the bottom of it.

"Isn't there a ritual or something? This doesn't feel very spiritual, just smoking in the bathroom like we're hiding from the principal. Don't we need to send the smoke to the heavens? This is not how I imagined it."

Rosemarie inhales and holds her breath. "This will change your thoughts," she says as she slowly exhales toward the sky. "Positive thoughts bring about positive change on the Earth. Here," she says, nudging me with the end of the pipe.

"I should tell you I have a fear of addictive substances. Addiction runs in my fam—"

"Just smoke it!" Zoe says, itching to get her turn and leaning her head on top of her forearms at the edge of the bathroom sink.

The smell is rich and fruity and mossy and earthy at the same time. I breathe it into the back of my throat and imagine the smoke swirling through the space between my brain and my skull. I imagine it turning into a wispy white ghost of a hand that coaxes all the negative energy from my cerebellum and blows it out through a hole in the top of my head. A smile instantly comes to my face, and I am lit. All of my synapses firing at once. Like the first time Danny held my hand.

"That's awesome," I say as I exhale. The smoke rises up into the dust-covered exhaust fan on the ceiling. I hope White Buffalo Woman can find it there.

Zoe smokes too. And we enjoy a moment of silence until Rosemarie's boss starts pounding the door down. This is funny to us for some reason, and we stumble out of the bathroom and run toward the car, waving good-bye to Rosemarie.

Even in the midst of our scrambling escape, when we step outside, nature has crystallized itself for me. I notice the sharp bright pins of the stars, the distinct shapes of the constellations, how they pierce the purple blue of the sky. I can smell the smoky piñon pine needles, the soft, flaking decay of the wood. I taste the dust of ancient rock. Feel the circumference of each tire as it spins and hurls us through space on I-90. I am pure sensation, and none of it is pain.

"Can you say 'peace pipe' ten times fast?" I ask Zoe as she steers the car with one hand, and we cross the border into Wyoming.

"Peace pipe, peace poyp, pee pah, pe . . ."

We break into hilarious laughter, tears pooling in the corners of our eyes, as Zoe begins to pass a red pickup truck trailing a red pony behind it in a white trailer.

"So much depends upon a red pickup truck trailing a red pony in a white trailer," she says, trying to parody the William Carlos Williams poem about the wheelbarrow that is senselessly thrown into every high school poetry anthology.

The driver is our age, it looks like, but he's actually wearing a Stetson hat. Without irony.

"Show him your boobs," Zoe says.

"What?"

"Well, all he can see is our heads, and they are not looking too good right now. Your boobs are perfect. Go ahead."

"He's wholesome."

"None of them are wholesome. There are straight men, and there are gay men, but there are no wholesome men. Write that down in your little notebook. Now show him your boobs. Say yes! Hurry," she says. She is approaching someone's taillights in the left lane and running out of time to keep flanking the pickup.

"Okay," I say, and Zoe honks the horn as I lift my shirt and press my nipples against the cold pane of the window. I use the bottom of my shirt to cover my face, so I can't see the wholesome cowboy's reaction to the Jersey girl's boobs hurtling next to him at eighty miles an hour.

It's strangely liberating. It's liberating, energizing, and thrilling to step outside all of the rules of decorum and exist in a place I've never dared to inhabit.

"Pull over," Zoe mouths to the cowboy, waving frantically at him.

I put my shirt down, bend over, and lay my head into my hands so he can't see me while the two drivers arrange some kind of rendezvous using only hand signals.

DESTINY

When I finally have the courage to sit up, Zoe is pulling up next to him in a parking spot behind a well-lit gas station.

"I can't believe you did it!" Zoe says as she parks the car.

"Why? Maybe I shouldn't have? Oh my god, what did I do?"

"No, it was perfect! Are you kidding me? Look at that guy. And his friend? They are actual cowboys."

Cowboys really do wear chaps, it seems. And soft suede gloves. And ropes wrapped diagonally across their chests. And they wear boots with spurs. They wear them right into the convenient parking lot of the gas station off I-90.

One gorgeous cowboy heads to each side of our car, and I wonder if they had a little powwow about which guy would get which of us. The driver of the pickup heads to Zoe's side, and I feel ashamed and rejected—he saw the boobs, after all—until I see the friend. Who is tall and shy and broad shouldered and blushing a little as he moseys on over to my side of the car.

"Evenin'," he says as he actually tips his hat back with the tip of his index finger and kind of shyly stares at me as he puts his hands on his hips. He looks like he's about to draw.

I can't stop nervous-laughing. "Where we come from," I say, "we dress like you for Halloween."

"And wherzat?"

I just look into his beautiful hazel eyes for a second. I don't understand what he is asking me.

"Wherzat where you are from?" he asks. He takes off his hat and holds it in front of his flat stomach, right above an enormous belt buckle shaped like a bucking bronco. It is a show of respect, which really isn't necessary since I've already flashed him my boobs, but I appreciate how polite he is. He says his name: "Dillon."

"Hannah," I say. "And I'm from New Jersey."

"City slicker, then."

"Not really, actually . . ." I am about to tell him what it's like where I'm from: the water-skiing, the autumn foliage, the blue jays, the spiky-finned sunfish, and the soft spongy green silt at the bottom of the lake, but I realize it would take too long.

It's chilly in the Wyoming night. His cheeks are getting rosy, and his breath issues forth in visible puffs when he talks. He has hair the color of a caramel apple and soft, thick eyelashes to match. If he were a girl, he could never find the right color mascara.

You would think his dense populace of freckles would be off-putting, but they have the opposite effect. They draw you in. They invite you to know him, because without them he would be inhumanly handsome.

"So do you guys actually wear this on a regular Saturday? Are those . . . Wait, turn around. Are those . . . Wranglers?" Zoe's beau, named Colby, backs up as she climbs out of the car to get a good look at him.

"I could ask you the same thing," he says, looking at Zoe's ridiculous-in-these-parts skimmer ballet flats. She is practically barefoot in the middle of frigid, muddy, dusty, manure-y Wyoming. They are pretty ballet flats, though, that she painted herself with a pattern of tiny polka dots. She's also wearing a beaded Native American pouch slung around her sideways and the big sleeping-bag coat from the nice ladies from Long Island.

Zoe looks down at her shoes and says, "'They are plant-like sieves not fit for the rainy night of America and the raw road night.'"

"She memorized *On the Road*," I tell Dillon.

"I see," he says.

"Is that for your gunpowder?" Colby asks about the pouch.

"Corn pollen, actually. It has magical powers."

"Where you ladies headed?"

"Yellowstone. We have to see a man about a buffalo."

"You came all the way from New York to see a buffalo?"

"Why not? We want to see one roaming. Outside of captivity. It needs to be a free buffalo and not one being led to slaughter to make hot dogs for some rich investment bankers suffering from ennui. Do you understand the word 'ennui'?" Zoe asks.

"Yes, ma'am. We take the SATs just like you."

"Do you vote for the Republicans and overuse fossil fuels and paper products?"

"I haven't yet had the privilege of voting, since I'm seventeen. But when it comes time to do it, I will study the candidates and make an informed choice."

"Because there are two very different visions of America right now, and you have to know which side you're on. It's like cowboys and Indians, and I'm afraid you'll be on the side of the cowboys. Since you, like, are one," says Zoe, lifting up and inspecting the hunk of turquoise holding together Colby's bolero.

"Don't judge a book by its cover, young lady," Colby tells her, pushing her hand away from the string around his neck.

"You mean there's such thing as a compassionate, intellectual cowboy?"

"Why don't you stick around and find out?"

Colby has his arm around her, and she's snuggled up into the crook of it. The girl acts fast. "So what can you show us? What do people do for fun in . . . where are we?"

"Outside Gillette."

"What do people do for fun in outside Gillette?"

"Line dancing. At the Wild Buffalo. And a little two-stepping."

"Take us there. We'll follow you."

"It would be our pleasure," Colby says, bowing and sweeping the hat.

"Look at that. Seldom a discouraging word," I say to Zoe.

"This one was a little discouraging about my corn-pollen pouch," she says, looking up at Colby and poking him in the ribs. By the look on the boy's face, he cannot believe his luck.

We follow them down the road a piece, horse trailer and all, to a huge barn-like establishment that vibrates with the tone of the bass and the treble of the caterwauling.

"You will like line dancing," Zoe says to me. "It's just following a lot of rules. And you keep your hands in your pockets. You don't have to worry about what to do with your hands. I know you worry about that."

"Is it that obvious?"

"Um . . . yeah."

"Doesn't sound like your thing, though. You don't like lines."

"I will be *interpretive* line dancing."

"Oh no."

"Fuck yeah."

"Oh god."

The cowboys come and open the doors for us and escort us, greasy hair and all, into the dance hall. It smells like buttered corn and barbecue sauce and the hay that is stuck to the bottom of people's boots.

"We need those," Zoe says, when she sees some hats for sale at the entrance, and she starts frantically pulling heavy rolls of coins from her corn-pollen pouch.

"Easy there," says Dillon. "We got it covered." They buy us some hats, so we look a little less grimy and we fit right in. And then: We dance.

It is a riot! Old ladies can do it, young men can do it. Everyone is out there doing it without shame or irony. I am doing it too! Stomping my heels and kicking my feet and maneuvering some intricate turns, all thankfully with my hands in the front pockets of my jeans.

Zoe's hands, on the other hand, are everywhere. She refuses to stay in line and instead spins and tiptoes and leaps between them. She doesn't disturb anyone, or interrupt their concentration; she simply does her own thing between the lines. Her arms are flailing and sweeping in big butterfly shapes, and her legs fan-kick in all directions. At one point I even see her rolling around on the floor with a dramatic Martha Graham look on her face. Poor Colby follows her around at first and then gives up and starts stomp-turning in line between me and Dillon.

A new song, a crowd favorite, comes on, and Dillon and

Colby are immersed in the lyrics and the steps. They forget about us for a second, and I hear Zoe *pssst*ing me near a big barn door at the side of the restaurant.

"Psst."

What? I mouth, and I throw up my hands. I am having a good time. I feel like I deserve a good time, and I am having a good time, and she starts *psst*ing me.

She waves me over, so I reluctantly leave my line and sneak over to the door.

"Come on," she says, pushing it open just enough for us to squeeze out into the cold dark night.

"What?" I ask her.

"You want to see a buffalo, right?"

"I guess, but I was having fun," I say.

She tiptoes up to the horse trailer, opens it, and starts backing the horse out.

"Tonight we ride," she says.

"Are you kidding me, Zoe?"

"What? You don't just want to drive up to a buffalo in a car. We will go rustle one up. We need an authentic buffalo encounter."

"Zoe."

"Hannah, trust me," she says, and I realize she is like ten steps ahead of me. We didn't pull the cowboys over to hang out with cowboys. We pulled them over to steal their horse and ride it into the Wild West.

She swings her skinny self up onto the horse and then grabs my wrist and helps me haul myself up behind her. The horse is very patient. We *clip-clop* out of the parking lot to the huge infinite expanse behind the bar. It's lit by the moonlight and the streetlamps, and it goes on for miles until it dead-ends into a shadowy mountain range miles and miles away in the distance.

We get onto the grassy field, and Zoe makes a clicking sound with her mouth like they do on TV, and then she kicks the horse with her heel, and he takes off. The cold breeze whips at our faces, and the spilling, tumbling, clomping of the horse's hooves pounds the earth. We're kicking up dust behind us, and it's like nothing I've ever experienced. The most free I've ever felt. At first I keep my face pressed against Zoe's back, and then when I hear Zoe yahooing, I yahoo too. I let go with one arm, whip it around in a circle as if I have a lasso, and I yahoo into the night.

After about ten minutes of this, Zoe pulls on the reins and slows the horse down to a slow trot. There is a small hill in front of us, and she points to it. "There. Over that ridge. We can probably see them from there."

"Really?" I ask. "Buffalo?"

I dismount, and Zoe slides off too.

"Zoe!" I whisper-yell.

"What?"

"A tumbleweed," I say. "Look!" I point to a dry beige vessel glowing in the moonlight. Its spiky thorns wrap around the emptiness, cradling it like a vase. "It's art," I say.

"It's beautiful," Zoe says.

We climb to the top of the ridge and peek over. We look down and see more miles of nothing.

Zoe seems a little defeated. Like she fully expected the field to be ass to elbow in buffalo. I don't know why she was so confident about it. "I could have sworn . . ."

"It's okay, Zoe. We saw a tumbleweed. That was cool enough."

"It's just a dead bush. Okay. Let's go. We have to return this horse. Maybe we'll see a buffalo tomorrow."

We ride back to the parking lot, where it seems Dillon and Colby have not even noticed us missing. They've probably already hooked up with some other girls. Easy come, easy go.

The horse keeps farting as we try to lead him back into his trailer and cover him with a blanket because that's what we've seen them do on TV. And we can't stop laughing.

As soon as we stop, he farts again, and we're laughing so hard we don't have the muscle control to finish the job.

"Okay, get serious," Zoe says. *[horse fart]* "We have to *[horse fart]* hook him into the front *[horse fart]* with the bungee."

"Ahaha. Ahaha . . . aha . . . Okay, I'm done laughing." *[horse fart]*

Eventually we get him in and lean up against the back of the trailer. We take some deep breaths to recover from the laughter, and then Zoe says, "Over there."

The bar is called the Wild Buffalo, after all, and in front of the parking lot stands a huge one made out of fiberglass. "I'll take your picture with him, in case we never see a real one."

"Okay."

Zoe pulls out the Polaroid she stole from Penn Station and snaps a photo of me on top of the rust-colored beast, and we get back in the LeMans and head toward Yellowstone, which, according to my Native sense of direction, is directly beyond Orion's belt.

We find a rest stop when we're tired, and we manually crank the seats back and look at the stars through the rectangular sunroof. It is a clusterfuck of stars. More stars than I've ever seen in my life, denser than the freckles on Dillon's face.

"I'm happy," I tell Zoe.

"I'm glad," she says.

"I don't know if it's the altitude or the clean air or stealing horses or what, but it feels like my esophagus and my heart and my stomach and my throat had been hog-tied for my whole life and someone has finally set them free."

"That's what this was about, little dogie. Setting you free. It's good to get away. And look at this . . ." she says, and she waves the Polaroid shot of me on the buffalo in front of my face.

"Whoa," I say, bringing it closer to my nose. There's me on top of the buffalo wearing the same outfit I've had on for three days, but with a cute cowboy hat on my head. I'm smiling, which is rare, and below me is an enormous shiny fiberglass buffalo. But it is white. "Maybe it was the flash," I offer.

"I don't think so. I think it is a sign. I think it is your destiny. You're destined to do something good here on this planet. Like white-buffalo good."

"Right," I say.

"Right. It is your destiny."

"Well, you can do something good too."

"Not here. My destiny is somewhere else. My destiny is bigger than the Earth. It's beyond it. Out there," she says pointing to the stars.

"You're going to be an astronautess?"

"No. We've been on divergent paths, my friend. For you, this trip was to help you find freedom, tap you into your white-buffalo goodness. I am trying to get back to them. I've been following them. Trying to catch up to them, and when we meet, they will take me with them."

"Zoe . . ."

"I don't expect you to understand," she says. "I don't want to force you to believe me. You don't have to believe in them. But I do. They will come for me."

"Zo . . . what you have—your condition—it sometimes makes you have big thoughts like that," I say. I honestly am flabbergasted. I thought she was getting better. The happy emotions I was feeling just minutes ago swirl around me and sink into a deep, vacuous, familiar black hole of worry. She is not healed.

"They showed me things," she continues. "They took my hunger away to study it. To figure out what makes humans tick. And little by little I am becoming one of them. I don't have to eat. I don't have to use the bathroom. Or sleep. I have nothing to lose by going with them."

"Noah," I say, finally pulling out all the stops. "What about Noah?"

Zoe turns away, almost visibly in pain. "He of all people will understand this. And you have to tell him about it. Tell him where I went."

"But I don't understand where you are going."

"It's an exoplanet. Around an M-dwarf star between the constellations of Cygnus and Lyra. There is life. But their lives are different than ours. Less dependent on physical bodies. They can convert themselves to energy. They can travel through lightning. I think they're trying to find me with all these wacky storms."

"But Zoe—"

"No 'buts.'"

"But . . ."

"You don't believe me."

"I just want to be a devil's advocate for a sec. If you do have something like bipolar disorder—"

"Which I don't—"

"You could have auditory and visual hallucinations. It's part of it. Your brain could just be misfiring a little. And these storms. They're part of climate change. They're what we have to get used to now in this new world we've created."

"You've known me my whole life, Hannah. And I wouldn't lie to you."

"I don't think you're lying."

"Whatever," she says, and I can see her start to shut down.

"Zo . . ."

"I am not crazy," she whispers.

And then she tries not to cry. She catches a sob in her throat, and I feel horrible. She is finally pared down to her true self, and I can't believe her. I can see her building a new wall, brick by brick, around herself. She takes a deep breath, sits up straight, and swallows the emotion. Her feeling of being entirely alone and misunderstood.

I can't take it anymore. "I believe you," I say. "I believe that you had some kind of experience. I truly do," I say. "But that doesn't mean that you have to run away. You can still make things work here. On Earth," I joke. "There are so many fashion-challenged earthlings who need you here. I need you here."

She laughs a little through her tears, before we try to get some sleep.

BETRAYAL

When we get to Yellowstone, we pull up to the park ranger booth and pay the entrance fee with some rolls of dimes that the park ranger insists on breaking open and counting. "Are you serious?" Zoe asks. "Each roll is five dollars. You're just going to have to roll them up again later."

The park ranger holds up her hand and says, "You made me lose count. I have to start again. Ten, twenty . . ."

Finally, we get some maps of the park and some literature that reminds us seventeen thousand times not to feed the bears or the buffalo. We drive along the curved wooded roads until we find an inclined meadow off the shoulder to our right. The frost has not yet melted off the grass, and there is some hovering loopy mist hanging low to the ground as if the earth is blowing smoke rings with a big earth cigarette.

We look for buffalo, but we don't see anything but grass.

"Let's go to Old Faithful," I say.

I am in way over my head. What I found out last night is

that there are limits to my faith in Zoe. They are at the outer limits of the galaxy, but they are limits nonetheless. Because I know too much about her past.

And because I've read at least thirteen case studies on bipolar disorder since her latest escapades. And in seven or more of the case studies, the patient experienced hallucinations involving talking to God. Or worse, being God. I think what happens is that when they are depressed, patients feel so worthless that the only way for them to get their self-esteem back is to exaggerate it. It becomes a habit, this grandiosity, until it gets out of control and bipolar people start to believe they are superhuman.

That hypothesis makes a lot more sense to me than Zoe actually having been abducted by aliens. She's just trying so hard to seem worthy. To herself, mostly. And trying to go somewhere where someone will appreciate her. I understand this, but I do not know what to do. So when she is digging through the rolls of coins in the backseat, trying to gather enough for some geyser souvenirs, I switch on my phone.

The irony of betraying Zoe in the parking lot of Old Faithful does not escape me. But in a way I am being faithful to her. I went about it the wrong way at first, but now I know she needs professional help.

I'm sure with the AMBER Alert, my phone number has been submitted to the police, and as soon as it's recognized that it's back on the grid and communicated to local authorities, we will be swarmed with rescue personnel. I imagine choppers and everything. But maybe this is my own grandiose thinking. We are not that important in the scheme of things.

We de-LeMans and I ask Zoe to go buy me some corn chips at the beautiful new visitor center that looks like a Swiss chalet ski lodge with a chevron-shaped window that frames the geyser perfectly if you want to watch it from inside.

I walk into the ladies' room and think I'm safe, since "alien Zoe" doesn't have to pee anymore, and I take a look at my phone. It is overwhelmed with voice mails, e-mails, and text messages. Surprising, though, is how many of them are from Danny. And my mom. She's written me page-long text messages apologizing and promising things will be different when I get home.

Danny has sent photos, though. Of him in his adorable sunglasses next to his ice cream truck. In Pennsylvania. Then in Chicago. And Iowa. The last one is at Indian City! With Rosemarie. Is he following us? He's got his long arm around her cushy shoulders, and they smile, Rosemarie's gold tooth glinting a little in the flash. I touch his crooked nose on the screen and trace his lips. I'm about to actually kiss my freaking phone, that's how in love I am with this boy, when Zoe yells into the bathroom.

"Hannah! Two minutes until she blows!" She stands outside my stall and leans against it waiting for me.

"Okay," I say. "Coming!"

"What are you doing?"

"Peeing."

"Well, hurry."

I am dying to text Danny and tell him where I am. It takes every ounce of energy for me to stand up, hide my phone in a deep inside pocket of my sleeping-bag coat, and step out of the stall.

"Come on," Zoe says as I wash my hands. I look at myself in the mirror. In the National Park, they discourage vanity. People should be focused externally—on the beauty and wonder of the natural world, and not on the size of their pores—when a miraculous geyser is about to blow, so they installed foggy mirrors that don't show the details of your face. I look at it anyway and try to see it the way Danny would. I am not as hideous as I often imagine I am. My eyes are intense, like my dad's, and my nose is not as big and pointy as I sometimes envision it. "Let's go!" Zoe says.

A huddled mass of travelers in primary-color parkas squeezes around the perimeter of the geyser. "We have to go over here. This place is crawling with webcams," Zoe says, so we stand in the farthest corner of the viewing area and wait for 10:37, the next eruption time according to a chalkboard beneath Old Faithful's name plaque.

A digital clock counts down the seconds. A park ranger with a microphone stops educating people about geothermal phenomena and turns our attention to the hole in the ground. The tourists focus their cameras, about to be amazed. Ten, nine, eight.

"I saw you turn on the phone," Zoe says without looking at me. She is staring at the pool where Old Faithful is supposed to erupt. Three, two, one.

Nothing happens. People stir. *Has this ever happened before? Can this happen? What does this mean?* Moms engage in nervous laughter as kids whine for justice. They traveled ten hours in the car for *this*? I hear them thinking.

Zoe is still staring with abnormal intensity at the pool, and then she reaches her hand toward it as if she's shooting it with some kind of invisible superhero ray. The ranger gets back on the microphone. "Ah, folks, um, this has never . . ." he says.

Zoe turns to me, winks, drops her hand, and Old Faithful erupts, white and queenly like a liquid statue of the Madonna, but twenty seconds off schedule.

When I turn back to Zoe, she is gone.

LOVE

I am numb—only energy, without a physical body, like Zoe's alien friends—as I sprint into the parking lot and try to figure out in which direction she fled. I know if she doesn't want to be found, though, Zoe will not be found. Already her weather radio, the turtle backpack with Tasery in it, and her corn-pollen sack are missing from the trunk. She also took $157 in coins. I know she is sprinting nimbly through the woods until she can find a kindly trucker to take her south through Colorado and Utah.

I'm out of breath, but I make one phone call before I turn it off again and hope that the authorities missed my temporary blip on the grid. Maybe they had even canceled the AMBER Alert. If they found out what Zoe did to Officer Franz, they may have decided we weren't worth retrieving.

"Danny!" I say breathlessly. "I lost her!"

"Where are you?"

His voice brings me back into my body. My hands quiver,

even now, itching to touch the muscles rippling beneath the soft cotton of his T-shirt. I shake them, trying to punish them for not staying focused on the crisis at hand.

"I lost Zoe," I say again.

For the first time in our lives, I let her down, and I let her down hard. It feels awful. It feels so awful I can't even feel. I'm still in shock. I want to cry, but there is a mask-like tightness around my eyes constricting my tears.

"I'm at Yellowstone," I say. "I think she's on her way south. She's chasing the weather."

"Okay. I'm right behind you. In Gillette. If you drive south to Buffalo, I'll meet you there, and we can continue on through Utah."

"What? How did you know where we were?"

"Zoe's been calling me."

"She has?"

"Every time you went to the bathroom, from a pay phone. She called first to ream me out. She was so pissed at me for hurting you that she had a few choice words for me. But I explained to her that the Rebecca thing has been petering out for months. I explained I wanted to see you. So a day later she began calling me every day. She just kept telling me that you were going to need me and that I should drive west on I-90. So I did. I really want to see you."

I was about to say "You do?" as if I didn't deserve his attention, but instead I say, "Me too. I think about you a lot."

"How much?"

Like every five seconds. Or more. Or continually. In the background of all my other thoughts is the perpetual thought of you, I think, but I don't say it out loud for fear of scaring him away.

He doesn't let me answer before blurting, "Meet me in Buffalo."

When I get to the gas station he told me to drive to, he stands there leaning against his ice cream truck in his sunglasses and barn jacket, like that iconic picture of James Dean. Only he's taller. And less perfect. And much more beautiful, in my opinion.

I park and try not to feel ashamed of my greasy unwashed blond hair as I walk over to him. I hug him and lean my cheek against his broad sculpted chest. He tilts my chin up, and I can feel him pressing against me as we kiss. The chemistry between us is animal. I can tell he can feel it too. Honestly, we haven't spoken more than 5,000 words to each other in our whole lives, but there's this whirling vortex inside me that needs to pull him into my body. Into my life.

"We have to go," I tell him as we break away. "We need to catch up to her."

"She's on foot," Danny says. "And I'm a fast driver." And then he smiles that smile that makes the corner of his eyes crinkle.

"Just a minute!" I say, putting a halt to it, imagining the sound of a needle scratching off an LP. "What about Rebecca? Is it really over? You were with her one hour after you left me that night. It took you one hour. You can't be alone for an hour to think about things before you crawl back into her lair?"

"She was waiting for me when I got home. I couldn't shake her. And how do you know this, anyway?"

"Never mind how I know. I know. She was with you when I called from Michigan too."

"We were doing homework."

"For sex ed?"

"Exactly," he says sarcastically. "We were doing our sex ed homework." He looks into my eyes. "It's over, okay? She's already moved on. I've moved on too."

"Really?"

"Yes."

He takes my coat off and lets it slide slowly down my back. Then he makes a bed with it between the ice cream coolers in the truck. We lie down together on our sides. He stares at me, moving his finger from my forehead, down my nose, over my chin, along my neck until it lands between my breasts.

"Oh look," I joke, "I'm wearing buttons."

"I see that," he tells me, and he uses his nimble fingers to deftly, expertly savor each one before he pops it open slowly.

There, in a parked ice cream truck just outside of Buffalo, Wyoming, I say yes. I resign myself to finding God. And it's true what they say. You can find God anywhere.

—

"Now, we have to go," I tell him. "Seriously." We're lying on top of the grimy nylon coat in the aisle of the truck. He is tracing his finger along the outside whorls of my ear.

He takes out his phone, holds it at arm's length, and takes a picture of us.

"Do you document all your conquests?"

"Nope."

It's then that we hear a knock on the door.

"Hannah Morgan," demands a sharp male voice.

Shit, I think. I thought this is what I wanted. Help from the authorities. But now that Danny's here, I have all the help I need. I don't want them to question me or send me home. I want to find Zoe.

We shuffle around getting dressed inside the truck.

"We need to ditch them," I tell Danny. "I thought . . ."

"Shh," he says, holding his finger to his lips. He stuffs his wallet into his pocket, walks to the back of the truck, and puts his hand on the big lever that opens the escape hatch in the back. The one you practice exiting from in safety drills on the school bus. He holds fingers up and silently counts. One. Two. Three. On three, he pushes the door open. We jump out of the truck and run fast.

"Stop!" the police officers say. "Stop in the name of the law."

They actually say that? I think.

"Serpentine!" I yell at Danny. I heard somewhere that you should run in a zigzag formation to avoid bullets. He smiles and yells, "No, just run straight for the highway!" We run through some brush across the access road and to the edge of the highway, where I see another tumbleweed. I don't have time to appreciate it, though. The overweight officers, dressed in tan, camouflaged in the dry landscape, are in hot pursuit. But we easily dodge the speeding cars on the highway with alacrity, and their cumbersome bodies can't keep up. We hear a horn whine and blare, and the screeching of brakes behind us. We keep going up an embankment on the other side of the road, and we run up and over another brown spiky bluff to the exit ramp on the other side.

A McDonald's looms ahead in the distance, but that's it. For miles. It looks like a McDonald's on the moon. Nothing is growing. No flora or fauna. And nothing is moving in any direction as far as we look. The landscape is completely mineral. We need a truck. Or a train or some kind of vehicle to jump upon.

Danny makes a dash for the McDonald's drive-through. And I follow him, though we'll be too easy to find, hiding in the only place to hide.

"Shouldn't we find a different McHidingSpot?" I ask him, panting for breath.

"I can maybe hot-wire one of those cars in the parking lot. Come on!"

I'm reluctant to steal a car. And I'm really reluctant to steal a car from a McDonald's employee whose entire paycheck goes into the upkeep of the car just so he can drive back to work. Like that story of Sisyphus rolling the rock up the hill and never getting anywhere.

"Can you make sure it's the manager's car?" I say as we run.

Danny just shakes his head and runs faster.

We squat down between a rusted-out old Honda Civic and a small, blue Ford pickup truck.

"Which one does my princess prefer?" Danny asks.

"The truck," I say. "Definitely the truck."

He wiggles something, and we're in.

There is one bench seat across the front, and it is shiny, vinyl, and hot. I slide in first. He looks beneath the steering column, finds the wires he needs, just like in the movies, and the truck sounds like it's clearing its throat for a second and then grumbles to life. Danny gets in, slams the heavy door, and puts on a baseball cap he finds in the front seat. "Get down," he says. "They're expecting two of us." I crouch down into the seat well, and he pulls slowly out of the parking lot so as not to draw attention to us.

I look up through the window into the side mirror and see the exhausted old cops finally arriving to the parking lot on foot.

"You're not eighteen, are you?" I ask him.

"Not yet," he says, and I hope that makes a difference in the penalty for grand theft auto. I hope the jury will understand how we needed the truck to rescue Zoe.

We drive south across the moon.

A little prism hangs from the rearview mirror, and it throws tiny rainbows around the cab as we drive. There is also a pair of pink fuzzy dice. "Do you think she would go to Vegas?" Danny asks, pointing at the dice. "I have a feeling about Vegas."

"I don't know," I say. "I need to hear a weather report. She has a thing about the weather." I lie down across the front seat and rest my head in Danny's lap as he drives, incognito in the hat and a pair of large sunglasses he also found in the truck.

I finally have time to reflect on the fact that I just lost my virginity and found God in the same moment. I've heard that doesn't usually happen.

He draws figure eights around my waist and then slides his hand beneath the waistband of my jeans and leaves it there. The proximity of my head to his "manhood," as they call it in romance novels, and the feeling of his whole hand on the soft skin around my hip make me want to pull over and find God again. It's addicting and more powerful than I ever imagined. No wonder salmon die, swimming upstream, leaping right into the open mouths of hungry bears by mistake.

"I like spawning," I tell him.

"I hope we didn't spawn anything," he laughs.

"We were careful. I want to be careful again," I say, sliding my finger down the inseam of his jeans.

"Easy there, killer. We need to put a little distance between us and the fuzz," he jokes.

"Can I sit up yet, then? I can't be touching you. It's driving me crazy."

"Wow, I created a monster."

"You don't feel it?"

"Of course I feel it," he says, looking at me. "I want to pull over and touch every inch of your naked body. Your armpit. The arch of your foot. The flat trail beneath your belly button. But I've been feeling it for five years, and I'm used to suppressing it."

"Why didn't you ever say anything? For five years? It would have made those five years a lot better for me. A *lot* better."

"I was afraid I'd scare you away. You are so studious and serious all the time."

"So why Rebecca Forman?"

"Practice girlfriend."

"What do you mean?"

"Someone to practice with. Develop some relationship skills."

"Did she know she was your 'practice' girlfriend?" I say, making air quotes. I never thought in a million years I could feel sorry for Rebecca Forman or pissed off at Danny Spinelli.

"No. She never needs to know that. We practiced with each other. She'll move on. She's tough like that. Besides, I taught her some mad skills." He laughs. "She can take them with her."

"But what if she fell in love with you? What if you broke her heart?"

"We never said 'I love you.' "

"But what if she secretly felt it?"

"I think she secretly felt love for someone else."

"Who?"

"Ice."

"Oh, they'd be perfect together."

"Right? So all's well that ends well. They've already gotten together. Which leaves me with no guilt. I am completely free and available to love you."

"Did you just say what I thought you said?"

"I said I was available to love you."

"But do you? Love me? We hardly know each other."

"I know you."

"You do?"

"I know that when you eat lunch, you're the only one in the cafeteria who actually places her paper napkin on her lap."

"So?"

"I know that you have a freckle right underneath your left eye. I know that when you smile, your eyes close into adorable half-circles and all that's visible are a little gleam of light and your thick black eyelashes. I know that you are really nice to that kid with Tourette's and you sit patiently and help him with his math homework even though he's uncontrollably barking 'cocksucker' at the top of his lungs every five minutes. I know that you are trying to improve your life even though the odds are stacked up against you, and that you hide in the attic of the Cunty Day School to try to learn as much as you can. I know that you would give your left arm to help Zoe if she needed it, and that's why we're here. I think I know enough."

"I've always known."

"What?"

"That I loved you."

"You came out of the womb loving me?" Danny jokes.

"Probably. I remember the day you came to the bus stop for the first time in kindergarten. I think I loved you then."

"That's kind of gross that you loved a five-year-old."

"Well, I was five too."

"I don't believe you loved me when you were five."

"Fine," I say, giggling.

"You are beautiful," Danny says.

"I feel lucky."

"You do? In the middle of Wyoming running from the law?"

"I do."

"Let's try your luck in Vegas, then, high roller."

ROMANCE

We drive another twenty miles, until it's safe to pull over at a diner called the Jackelope. The jackelope is a mythical creature in these parts. Part jackrabbit, part antelope; a taxidermist creates it by putting some horns on the rabbit. Since taxidermy seems to be a theme of this adventure, I think it's a good omen, and we choose it as a place to stop and regroup. I even wonder if Zoe stopped here as well. I get a weird tingly Spidey sense that she has been here before us.

The gift shop is cluttered with western crapola, but luckily they do have a 1998 road atlas for sale. I buy it with the last roll of nickels I have in my pocket, and I open it up in the diner, where I order an egg-white omelet with mushrooms and a short stack of blueberry pancakes.

Danny stares as I put the meal away, with some slow, methodical shoveling of my fork.

"It's been a while since I've eaten," I explain with my mouth full. "Zoe isn't really motivated by food these days."

"I love a girl with a big appetite," he says.

"Well, that's good for the both of us. Here," I say and I hold out a bite of pancake for him.

I look at the Wyoming page of my atlas and measure out the miles between us and Las Vegas with the bent-up part of my forefinger between the second and third knuckle.

"What are you doing?" Danny asks.

"Measuring. The distance between your second and third knuckle is approximately an inch, and it's thirty miles per inch on this map."

"Everyone's forefinger is the same size between the second and third knuckle?"

"Approximately. We have an inborn uniform standard of measurement."

"Is that how they discovered the 'inch'?"

"Maybe. And then a 'foot' must be the average length of a person's real foot."

Speaking of feet, Danny has taken off his shoes under the table, and he is slowly sliding his foot up and down my calf beneath my pant leg.

"Um," I say, trying to ignore him. "Can you ask them if they have the Weather Channel on that TV?"

He politely summons our waitress and asks her to turn on the Weather Channel while I map out the quickest route to Vegas. We basically have to shoot diagonally across the entire state of Utah. And part of it is through the Rockies, so we'll need to make sure it's not snowing. I hear it's suicide to drive through the Rockies in a snowstorm. People have been buried alive in their cars and forced to eat their pets or their belts. Maybe that's an urban legend, but I don't want to take the chance.

When the weather map comes up on the TV screen, it thankfully shows no storms through Utah, but the weather-caster, a woman in a red dress with a matching long red jacket, points to Vegas and warns about a weather "event" containing unusual amounts of lightning moving from west to east across the southwest United States. "We don't know yet what to call it," she says. "We're waiting for it to take shape and define itself, but for now, we've issued a general storm warning for all of Clark County, Nevada."

Danny has somehow worked his sock-covered foot all the way up to my seat between my legs, and I'm massaging it underneath the tablecloth.

"Danny!" I say, coming to my senses.

"Let's go to the bathroom," he says, pointing his head in that direction.

"Together? That's too advanced," I joke. "I'm new at all this, remember?"

"Okay," he says, nudging me once more with the foot.

"Plus we have to get there," I say, pointing to the lightning-covered map, "before that storm does. I'm afraid of what she might do."

"How far is it according to your knuckle?" he asks.

"At least twenty more knuckles. If we don't hit traffic or weather or whatever."

"How bad could traffic be in Utah?" he asks. "Do Mormons even drive? Or do they do the thing with the horse and buggy like the Amish?"

"They drive, you idiot. And you totally just jinxed us about the traffic."

We pay the bill and buy a jackelope to give to Zoe when we find her. Danny has brought all of his ice cream man money with him, and he's burning through it pretty quickly. It kills me thinking of the big box of coins sitting on the floor of the LeMans. I hope the cops have saved it for evidence and haven't pilfered it to do loads and loads of their laundry.

We leave without visiting the bathroom together, but in five miles Danny finds a deserted rest area, where he parks behind a tree and I climb on top of him in the driver's seat.

"Okay, that's it!" I say when we are done. "We need to focus on Zoe. No more of this until you bring me Zoe," I joke.

"I know you're new to all this, but you should never use sex as a bargaining tool," he says jokingly.

"I'm using it as a reward."

"I guess that's okay then," he says.

We get back on the road and drive through Utah, where everything is the Crayola crayon color Burnt Umber and the sky is Cornflower Blue. The rock formations and the crested buttes are absolutely fabulous.

"Erosion is my new favorite artist," I say.

"Erosion rocks," Danny says. "There's a joke in there somewhere, but I haven't perfected it yet."

We're both so unaccustomed to so much space. It's liberating and intimidating, and it's making us giddy. We feel overexposed. Compared to this place, our home seems like a little village in a train set. Everything at home is miniature and green and close together, which makes it seem quainter.

Nothing here is quaint, I think, looking out the window.

I take a little nap, and then we switch, and I drive the rest of the way to Vegas while Danny sleeps.

Every once in a while, I glance over at his face. His five o'clock shadow is beginning to grow, but it grows in uniformly and just serves to shade and accent his best features. His chin is perfectly squarish. A chin is very important, I realize, in my very subjective estimation of masculine beauty. It has to be pronounced and squarish, but not so big that you can grab it like a handle. He has a perfect chin, and his hair is growing longer and curlier and blacker, less Brillo-y now that it's long, and more inviting to the touch. I want to feel those curls wrapped around my fingers.

I wake Danny up when I get to the Strip because no one should miss their first ride into Vegas. Three in the morning is probably the perfect time to arrive here. The retro, iconic

WELCOME TO FABULOUS LAS VEGAS NEVADA sign is lit up in its full glory—even though it's a little-known fact that the Strip is actually located in a town called Paradise, Nevada, and not Las Vegas at all.

Everything is illuminated. Some big old grumpy father in the sky is looking down on Vegas and yelling, "Don't forget to turn off the lights!" It makes sense that Zoe's alien friends would meet her here, because it's probably the only town that's visible from space.

Billboards and marquees advertise comedy shows, washed-up vocalists, bands from the eighties, French circuses, wedding chapels, tattoo parlors . . . In the periphery, we can see mini landmarks from around the world. The Eiffel Tower, the pyramids, the Empire State Building, the Venice canals.

"This is quite the spectacle," Danny says groggily.

"You said it," I say, cruising at ten miles per hour in proper cruise position, with my forearm leaning against the open window of the pickup truck. Which—we found out after searching through the glove compartment—belongs to a man by the name of Samuel Rodriguez. We have every intention of returning his vehicle to him as soon as possible. Danny even wrote him a postcard from the Jackelope diner.

We search for Zoe.

The only way to distinguish the whores from the bachelorettes, bingeing on their last night of freedom, is that the whores can walk properly in their seven-inch Jimmy Choos. The others stumble around twisting their ankles, boobs falling out of their halter tops, lips stained red from too much cheap red wine. It's ugly. Their drunken bridesmaids stumble after them, wearing some kind of uniform trinket on their heads. I didn't realize until now that I had such strong feelings about bachelorette parties. They just represent everything that's wrong with this country. The shameless exhibitionism, the complete inability to embrace moderation.

It's because we're sort of looking for Zoe that we keep finding more whores and bachelorettes. Maybe we wouldn't notice them as much if we weren't looking for a young woman.

We also notice the homeless kids. Vegas is a runaway mecca because it's so easy to get lost here. Which is strange because these kids are not inconspicuous. They seem bent on attracting attention, actually, with their neon-colored hair and silver studs everywhere, begging passersby for $6.99 to take advantage of the cheap casino prime rib special. I stare at a doughy, green-haired white girl in a men's vest. She's slumped against a storefront playing some kind of game, trying to toss the coins she's collected into a plastic cup. I try to imagine how different she must look from her yearbook photo.

"Look, the 'World's Biggest Gift Shop,'" I say, changing gears.

"Look, 'Skintight 2000: A Spectacular Revue for Mature Audiences.'"

"That counts us out," I say.

"You said it," Danny replies, and then, "There!"

"Where?" I ask and I follow his pointing finger.

A young woman in silver lamé leggings, a purple leather studded halter that stops way before her belly, and six-inch hot-pink heels sits on the curb, with her perfect legs bent up on either side of her. She looks like David Bowie from *Ziggy Stardust*, but with a darker complexion and straight American teeth. She holds her silver head in her hands, and I'm praying she's not looking into a pool of her own vomit.

"Zoe!" we both scream out the passenger-side window. I look for a place to pull over, and the closest thing is the beginning of the circular driveway of the Venetian, a monstrous resort that is almost the size of Venice itself. The tower is so big it looks like another wonder of the world, like the Hoover Dam or the Great Wall of China. It is definitely visible from space.

We clamber out of the vehicle and rush toward her.

"Zoe!" I say. "Thank god!"

"Guyz," she says, looking up at us with red-rimmed eyes and severely dilated pupils. She stares at us blankly and seems confused about where she is and what she is doing here. She is trying to sit still but can't help moving back and forth in a slow swaying motion.

"What are you doing?" I ask her.

"Jus takin a res," she slurs, about to lie down on the sidewalk.

"No, Zoe. Not there."

"Where can I take a res?" she asks.

"She's drunk," I say. "I've never seen her drunk."

"No. Not drunk. Just in diabetic shock," Zoe corrects me.

"You're not a diabetic."

"Okay," she says, giggling, "then I'm drunk."

"I'm not surprised. You haven't been eating enough to tolerate any alcohol at all," I say, sitting down next to her.

"Here," Zoe says pointing emphatically to the ground, "in this place, there is alwaysz a party."

"Do you know where 'here' is?" Danny asks.

"Of course. Las Vegas, Nevada. Oooo. Les get tattoooos."

"No."

"Yes. Tattoos. Now," she says, pouting a little like a toddler. "Either we get tattoos, or you two," she clumsily points at us, "get married."

"No tattoos tonight. I'm putting my man-foot down," Danny says.

"Man-foot." Zoe laughs. "You have to be a man to have a man-foot. Are you going to let him talk to me like that?" she asks me.

Danny helps me hoist her to her feet, where she towers over both of us in the outrageous heels. Her belly is completely bare, and she has the corn-pollen pouch from Rosemarie slung across her body. It is bulging and heavily weighted with what's left of her coins.

"I'm the tallest. I get to say what we do. Les get tattooz," she says, spitting a little with the *t*'s.

"We are doing nothing until I get a shower," I say.

"Yeah," Zoe says, looking me over. "Good idea."

"I don't think we can afford this place, though," Danny says, pointing at the Venetian.

"You'd be surprised," I tell him. I'd rescued my father from enough Atlantic City casinos to know that hotel rooms here are cheap. They just lure you in, so you'll blow your cash gambling. They could give hotel rooms away for free. It's the gambling that sustains them.

We left the pickup truck running because we didn't want to have to hot-wire it again to restart it. When we get to the car, with Zoe hobbling next to me, leaning on my shoulder, Danny and I both realize the same thing at the same time. We can't valet park the Samuel Rodriguez pickup. What would we do when they ask for a key? So we try to find the only meter in Vegas and stumble upon it right across the street from the Venetian.

"See, we're lucky already," I say.

We walk back up the Venetian driveway, carrying nothing but the jackelope we bought for Zoe. I don't know where she left the rest of her things—her big coat, her turtle backpack with the weather radio and Taser in it—and I don't think she does either. I have a feeling she traded them for her current ensemble.

"They have Italy here," Zoe slurs as she points to the network of turquoise chlorinated canals around the entrance. "I think they bought it."

"Yes," I say. *God, she's losing brain cells quickly*, I think.

The inside is filled with Titianesque fresco paintings of Roman warriors and the backs of plump, naked ladies. It is so ornately decorated with golden architectural details, I don't know where to look.

"It'z so opulent," Zoe says.

"If by 'opulent' you mean 'gaudy,'" Danny answers. His Jersey accent comes out a little on the word *gaudy*, and it gives me a little tingle. *He has taste*, I think, which many people don't realize is a different thing than having money.

"It looks like Donald Trump threw up in here," I say. "And where is the front desk?"

The whole first floor is basically a shopping mall surrounding the indoor shallow pools, which I refuse to keep calling "canals."

"I didn't know Venice was a mall," I joke. "Or that the canals were so blue."

"Let'z go for a ride on the long boat thing." Zoe points across the shallow pool to where the motorized gondolas are covered and parked for the evening.

"It's closed, Zoe," I say.

"This place," she says, pointing again emphatically to the ground, "this place never closes."

She uses her long silver legs to climb over a railing in a single bound and then splashes into the water. She begins wading toward the gondolas.

"Zoeee!" I whisper-yell. "Zoe, get out of there."

"See," Zoe is saying. "Iss not closed. Iss just self-service after midnight."

"Danny," I say, looking desperately in his direction, and he vaults the railing, wades out to Zoe, and sweeps her into his arms in one fell swoop. Zoe kicks her feet a little, but she doesn't put up too much of a fight as he carries her back to land.

We dry her off with Danny's barn jacket and drag her to the front desk. A kind, short-haired man named Amand awaits. You can tell he was taught to be patient with folks like us at his hospitality college.

"Good morning, folks. How can I help you?" he says as Zoe slams the jackelope down on the front desk and pets it on top of the head.

"We need a room for the night," Danny answers.

"Sure thing. Can I interest you in our Romance Package? For just fifty dollars extra, you get two gondola rides and two tickets to the wax museum."

Zoe is leaning with one elbow on the front desk and says,

"We need three." She points clumsily at all three of us. "She loves him, and I love her, so we want three tickets in the Romance Package."

"Um, it comes with two," the polite man says.

"But there are all kinds of love, and you can't diszcriminate. Three tickets."

Danny says, "It's okay, Zoe. You can have my ticket to the museum."

"No, Danny. It'z the prinziple. They shouldn't put our love"—again she drunkenly points to the three of us—"in a box."

The clerk points at me. "Is your love for her romantic?" he asks.

Zoe takes a moment to consider this. "No," she says. "But that doesn't matter. I love her. So I should get a ticket too."

"It's called the 'Romance' Package."

"Well, what kind of package do you have for our kind of relationship? If you don't have one that suits us, then you are discriminating against our love."

"Sir, I'm sorry," I say. "Zoe, just let him do his job."

"I'll just give you three tickets," the clerk says. "It's okay."

"See," Zoe says. "The squeaky wheel . . ." She turns around and leans on the desk with her shoulder blades while she examines her fingernails, and the clerk hands us our keys.

Our hotel room is a standard one with two beds and

stripey polyester maroon bedspreads. The cheaply framed prints on the wall depict abstract ink drawings of gondoliers. Zoe flops on the bed face first and spread-eagle while Danny jumps in the shower.

Her face is buried in the nasty Las Vegas hotel comforter, and I begin to slide it out from under her so at least she is plastered into a clean sheet.

"You are protecting me from the spermatozoa," she says into the bed.

"Among other things," I say.

"Stop protecting me."

"It's what I do. I like protecting you."

She rolls over and looks at the spiky spackled ceiling as if she's finding shapes in the clouds. So I lie perpendicular to her, with my head resting on her stomach.

"I see a mermaid," I say.

"Where?"

"There. See the tail?"

Zoe snaps a picture of it with her Polaroid that she had placed on the nightstand. "Remember when you thought you saw a sea monster in the lake?" she asks.

"I could have sworn . . . But I guess it was just a piece of driftwood."

"And you set up video cameras at the end of the dock. You were so determined."

"Part of me still thinks it was a sea monster . . . Remember when you lived for twenty-four hours inside that squirrel hole in the big tree?"

"I didn't want them to cut it down."

"I think I do know what I want, Zo. From life. I'm afraid if I tell you, though, it will jinx the whole thing."

"Then keep it to yourself. But write it down somewhere. Make it real in some small way."

"Okay," I say, and I draw a little heart on the inside of her wrist with the pen I found next to the Gideon Bible in the nightstand.

LUCK

At noon the next day, Zoe is much better, and we eat the breakfast included in our Romance Package for three. Then we head downstairs to the casino. Zoe doesn't want the jackelope to suffocate, so she carries him in a plastic laundry bag with his head sticking out of it. The convenient shopping mall in our hotel has allowed us to find her some more-appropriate travel clothes: some black leggings and a big LAS VEGAS sweatshirt. I am still wearing my ensemble from the Walmart in Ohio but have sprung for some clean underwear, and I wear them out of the dressing room at Victoria's Secret and hand the tag to the cashier.

Apparently I am not the first person to have done this, because she is completely unfazed and tells me to have a nice day.

"Okay, time to go, folks," I say, swinging my dirty underwear back and forth in my pink VS shopping bag. "Let's get back to the East Coast."

The two of them stop in their tracks and stare at me like I'm insane.

"What?"

"What do you mean, 'what'? We're in Vegas."

They're both practically panting at me like they're two little pugs and I'm holding a pork chop.

"Two hours," I say. I need to get Zoe strapped into a seat belt in Samuel Rodriguez's pickup before she takes off again.

The two of them practically jump up and down and head to the casino.

I thought I was going to have a seizure from the noise and the lights, but somehow all the clinking and clanging begins to morph into white noise, and you stop noticing it after a while.

Danny climbs behind me on my stool in front of a slot machine. He is straddled behind me, and I feel the heat of him penetrating my body in electric waves. I help him make his bets and push the buttons while Zoe works the machine next to us. When we win, he kisses me on the neck. We gamble away the $157 in coins that Zoe brought with her from Yellowstone. It is amazing how quickly we go through it and how energized we are from the extra oxygen they pump into the room to keep you awake.

When we get to our last token, Danny holds it up, we all kiss it, and . . .

We win the jackpot!

Lights, sirens, bells, and whistles go off as the quarters keep clanking into the metal tray in front of us. A heavy, glorious, silver rain.

"I told you you were lucky," Danny whispers in my ear, kissing it.

We win $650.

"Just enough for tattoos," Zoe says. "To symbolize and memorialize our good fortune!"

"No, Zo. I thought you let go of that idea."

"Nope. We get tattoos, or you two get married. Because we're in Vegas, and we should do something wild. What have I taught you about audacity and saying yes?"

Maybe it's the extra oxygen in the air, but I do say yes, on the condition that she agrees to come home with us as soon as the ink is dry.

It doesn't hurt as much as I thought it would. You just have to get used to the perpetual scratching sensation.

We get tiny lucky horseshoe tattoos on the back of our right upper hips. So we can hide them if we want or show them with some low-rise jeans or in a bathing suit. "It's good to have options," Zeke, our ink master, tells us. He has no options left, it seems, because his entire body is covered. He even has a goddess on the back of his arm who gets pregnant when he bends his elbow.

The horseshoes are cute, and Danny likes it too. It will remind me of our journey west, stealing horses and making friends with cowboys.

Zoe snaps some photos of my ink. I'm actually happy we did it, although it felt a little like deciding to get pregnant. Like, once the needle touched my skin, there was no turning back. There are very few irreversible decisions in this life, and getting a tattoo is one of them. Semi-irreversible, anyway. And that was the eeriest part about it.

Danny opts out of getting inked himself, which I'm happy about. I like him just the way he is. We go to Madame Tussaud's then, and aside from the faux celebrities' flat, matte complexions, the likenesses are astounding. We show our tattoos to wax Leonardo DiCaprio, wax Will Smith, wax Zac Efron, and wax Michael Jackson.

"Blue Man Group?" Zoe asks when we're done. "They're playing in this hotel."

"I don't like art for the sake of art," Danny says, and I'm surprised and thrilled that he has opinions about art at all. "Art should say something, or move people or at least demonstrate some kind of special skill of the artist. That show is just guys in blue makeup spitting bananas at the audience."

"Well, maybe some people are moved by spit bananas," Zoe says.

"Maybe. I'm not going, though." Danny takes his share of

the jackpot to try to win some more in the casino while Zoe and I sit in the replica of San Marco Piazza.

"The real one has pigeons," I tell Zoe.

"It's probably unsanitary to do that here."

"But I think that's the coolest thing about the Piazza. The pigeons and how you can feed them. And how they land on your head. Without pigeons, it's just a big flat space."

We realize we are both leaning to the left to avoid sitting on the now-sore tattooed side of our butts, and we crack up. We move the left sides of our chairs together so we can lean into each other and have a conversation.

"Why did you do that to yourself last night?" I ask her.

"I was trying to forget."

"Forget what?"

"That you don't believe me. And that I have nothing to go home to. I don't even have a home anymore."

"You do, Zo. You have your mom and Noah. They love you. They need you, Zoe."

"But don't you get it? You are my home, Hannah. And if I don't have you, I have nowhere to go."

"You have me."

"No I don't."

"You do. What do you mean? I'm right here, leaning next to you on my left butt cheek."

"I was abducted by aliens, and they want to travel through the lightning and take me with them."

"I know that's what you believe."

"But if you don't believe it, that means you think I'm crazy. And I can't live with that."

"Zo. *Crazy* is the wrong word. What if you just tried the lithium? Just to see how it made you feel? To see if it evened you out."

"I can't believe you don't believe me."

"Can't you see, though, that you're asking a lot?"

"It's not supposed to matter how much I ask. We took an oath."

"But I think maybe in the fine print, it says that I can try to get you help if you need it."

"I don't need it. It's not my fault that they chose me. They liked the museum I made for Noah, I think. It helped them understand things about us. Or it was just my luck. Sometimes luck can be bad, you know. That's my lesson about luck."

"You're preaching to the choir on that one, sister."

And she's right, because just then Danny comes to get us and tell us that a bunch of cops have surrounded Samuel Rodriguez's pickup truck.

TRUTH

"Maybe we should just turn ourselves in," I say.

"Have you learned nothing on this trip? I don't think I've been teaching about giving up," says Zoe.

"It actually will look better if we go home on our own recognizance," Danny says to me.

"That's good, the recognizance thing. You can do that after I make one more stop," Zoe says. She points to a television screen across the Piazza, because a person can't possibly sit in a piazza without watching some TV, I guess. It's tuned to the Weather Channel and the weatherperson points to a swirling red storm in a giant paisley shape hovering over the Grand Canyon. "You want to see the Grand Canyon, don't you, Hans?"

The storm Zoe was chasing had apparently bypassed Vegas and is headed straight for Flagstaff.

"Why would I take you there, Zo? What are you going to do?"

"I just want to show you the truth. You can see for yourself."

"Let's just go home, Zoe. Enough is enough. I got the tattoo." It was still sore, and in spite of the antibiotic ointment and Band-Aids I covered it with, it keeps rubbing against the waistband of my jeans, and it's driving me crazy. "It's time to go back and face the music. It'll be good. We can start over. Clean slate," I say.

"They're just going to put me back in the hospital," Zoe mumbles.

"Maybe not," I say.

"I'm starting to feel bad."

"About what?"

"Amy Winehouse. Janis Joplin. Jimi Hendrix. Jim Morrison. Babies with cancer. Dying young. Drowning polar bears. Fundamentalists. Sex slaves. Orphans. Boy soldiers. Lonely middle-aged bachelors who live with their moms. Our pathetic parents. Especially Amy Winehouse. Why didn't anyone save her?"

"That is sad," Danny says.

I pull my finger across my throat, indicating for him to stay out of it.

"If we go to the Grand Canyon, I will stop feeling bad. We can run away from the badness."

"No, we have to face the badness."

"After the Grand Canyon."

"Now, Zo."

And before I can tell Danny to grab her, she takes off. She runs, with the jackelope under her arm, through the mall of the Venetian and out the back door of the food court. She dodges a bunch of Dumpsters, gets to the Strip, and takes a left. Danny takes long strides behind her, but she ducks into a casino, and we lose her in the cacophony of the crowd.

"Shit," he says. "She's a slippery little minx."

"This way," I say. I remember seeing a runaway camp under the highway a few blocks away. And knowing Zoe, she has probably made friends with a bunch of other runaways. Not that we're runaways ourselves. We're just on vacation, I remind myself.

We find them under a bypass. Their camp consists of some cardboard boxes, a couple of dirty old hotel bedspreads, and two fuzzy chairs shaped like leopard-print, high-heeled pumps.

The runaways are pierced and greasy and smoking and feeding Dumpster pad Thai to their pet stray dog, who is tied to a rope.

"Have you seen our friend Zoe?" I ask the one who seems like the leader. She has pink hair and combat boots and looks significantly unwashed.

"She the Silvery Jersey Girl?"

"Yes."

"Right on."

Danny hates it when people say "right on." It's so Orange County. "Have you seen her?" he insists.

"Not today."

"What would she do if she were trying to get to the Grand Canyon?"

"She could pawn something to get bus fare, stop at the Homeless Youth Center, or join a hotel tour. That would take some research, though, to find out which ones are leaving when. And they probably stop at the Hoover Dam first, which would be a waste of time. She have anything to pawn?"

"A jackelope?" I say tentatively.

"That might catch a fair price. People love their kitsch around here, if you haven't noticed," she says, pointing to the shoe chairs.

"I see that," I say. "My name's Hannah, and this is Danny."

"I'm Joan," she says, but her real name is probably Madison or something. I think briefly about the parents of a girl named Madison who has turned into this person named Joan. All the good intentions gone awry. I wonder what they did to her to make her want to leave and live here beneath the highway. It must have been something terrible. No one is that much of an ingrate. No one would leave a comfortable home and live here unless something bad was happening. That's why they're called runaways. Because there's something they needed to get away from.

"Well, thanks for the info," I say.

"Pawnshop is on Fremont."

When we finally find it, we know Zoe's gone because the jackelope is already in the front window wearing a Rudolph nose and a tiny Santa hat. The pawnbroker is blaring "Silver Bells," my father's favorite Christmas carol, and I can't think of a more spiritless place to cultivate the Christmas spirit: a pawnshop in Vegas in the middle of a desert without even a hint of a chill in the air. The song makes me want to go home. I tear up a little. I feel like I want my mom. Which is a primal feeling, but one that I've trained myself to stop feeling since I turned fourteen and she got so depressed.

"I want to go home," I say to Danny, and I let him hug me while I cry. I even want to see my dad, I think. As fucked up as they are, I never once doubted that they loved me. They wanted me. And that is worth something. That may be worth trying to fix. "I really want to go home." I wipe my nose on my sleeve. "I'm sorry," I say. "I cry sometimes when I'm tired."

"So let's go. Let's get out of here."

"I can't go home without her, Danny."

"Okay." He sighs. "I saw a Greyhound station on Main Street. Let's do this thing."

The thought of a Greyhound bus—the nauseating rocking sway, the sickly sweet smell of the commode chemicals sloshing around in the back, the ultra-cool blast of the air conditioning—makes my stomach turn.

"What about the airport?"

"We couldn't get through security."

"Oh yeah."

"How much trouble are we going to be in for stealing that car?"

"Teenagers, first offense, joyride, no intention of keeping it. We might get off with community service. But this is the culture of the car. And they punish you severely for screwing with someone's vehicle. I think it may be worse than assault and battery."

The reality of our situation is sinking in, and I feel hopeless and shaky for a moment. Like I've had seven cups of coffee. I breathe in. And breathe out. And try to think of a plan. It's easy to choose, though, because we have no choice. We have to get to the Grand Canyon.

It's a six-hour bus ride with two bathroom breaks and a break for a meal. Zoe is not here at the bus station, though, and there was no earlier bus. I have no idea how she's going to get there, but I know she's going to get there, so we buy our tickets in time for the 5:00 P.M. departure.

Danny buys some pretzels, cheese crackers, and a Coke. "Whatever you want, my lady. It's on me," he says with a grand gesture toward the row of vending machines along the back wall of the station. He still has ice cream man money left, and he won a little more at the slots while I was talking to Zoe in the Piazza.

I choose some trail mix and popcorn and some Fig Newtons for dessert.

"Nice, that has, like, all the food groups. You got some protein and fruit and carbs and fiber."

"I try," I say. "Nutrition is interesting to me. Even in the most challenging of circumstances."

"Is that what you want to study?"

"I never thought about it, but that might be a good option."

"People need help with that. You could make a change."

And, then, since we're in Vegas, one of MJ's favorite towns, we start singing "Man in the Mirror."

"My mom liked Michael Jackson," Danny admits.

"But you didn't?"

"Well. He may be a guilty pleasure. What's yours?"

"I like romantic comedies."

"All girls like romantic comedies. That's not embarrassing."

"Yeah, but I feel guilty about it. They're so predictable. They always end with proclamations of love made in the fake rain. Why do they always do the rain thing?"

"I don't know. It's a symbol, I guess. Of how love conquers all. Even the weather."

"Do you believe that?"

"I refuse to answer on the grounds it may incriminate me."

"No. It's okay," I say. "How can anyone grow up with *parents* and still believe that love conquers all? What teenager on the planet has parents who are still in love?"

"My grandparents are still in love."

"Really?"

"Yup, and they're eighty-three. They got married when they were our age, and they're still together. He still goes on about how beautiful she is to him. And how he remembers the day he first saw her."

"Are they in the *Guinness Book of World Records*?"

"No"—he laughs—"but maybe it's still possible. For love to conquer all. Maybe love ebbs and flows and just goes through a deep trough when your kids are teenagers. You either stick it out or you don't."

Just then our bus pulls up. The dreaded bus. I look around at our fellow travelers. Just some old guy wearing an Indian-blanket poncho, carrying an Incan pipe flute and a suitcase full of his CDs to sell to the tourists at the Grand Canyon. We heard him playing in San Marco Piazza, his haunting, ancient tune evoking the mysteries of his steep, thin-aired Peruvian homeland. We also heard him, or one of his brothers, in Chicago . . . and Yellowstone, now that I think of it. His eerie whistle has become the ubiquitous soundtrack for this adventure.

It starts to rain then; the storm we've been promised has finally broken. It rains hard and sudden. We can learn a lot from the desert. How it patiently waits to be nourished. And then doesn't waste what it's been given. It's a grateful little ecosystem that's conservative with its resources.

It hardly ever rains in the desert, though, so when it does, it deserves some ceremony. We honor the rain by enacting our own final scene from a romantic comedy. I wait in front of the bus holding a newspaper over my head while Danny pounds on the window of the bus station. "Wait!" he mouths. "Don't go!" and then he runs out and picks me up and spins me around. I act surprised when he kisses me, and we get soaking wet together in the teeming rain as we're standing in front of the Greyhound bus to Flagstaff.

"Tickets, please," the driver says. He was not amused by our performance. We hand him our tickets and take a seat near the front so I won't have to smell the bathroom.

It's a long ride through more crazy moon-like landscapes, and because our driver is a madman hauling the bus at ninety miles an hour, we stay just ahead of the storm, which is following behind us like a big black blanket, threatening to tuck us in for the night.

We stop in two little towns where the houses all look like Taco Bells, and I wonder what it would be like to live out here in a little Taco Bell house in the "dry" heat so far away from a big body of water. It makes my freshwater self panic a little. What do people do without the city or the lake or the ocean to go to? It's just land, land, and more land.

They play golf, I guess, and tennis, and they go to the

mall or do "basketball choreography" like the happy kids from *High School Musical* who also dance on the tables of their outdoor cafeterias. This makes me laugh.

"What?" Danny asks.

"I think I have another guilty pleasure. I think I like musical theater."

"Ouch," Danny says. "We'll have to work on that one." He takes my hand, and I feel his touch throughout my entire body. I lean over and kiss him, and he asks me for an eight-letter word for *truth*. He bought a book of crosswords at the bus station, and he's determined to finish this puzzle before kissing me for real.

"Veracity," I say.

"Ooh, you're good."

"There's not much else it could be. Not a lot of words for *truth*. Because there is only one. Truth."

"I think there could be different versions of truth," he says. "You choose your truth, and then you build your life around it."

"Give me an example."

"So, Rebecca Forman."

"Yeah?"

"Objectively, empirically, she is not pretty. She has a big nose. Her eyes are too close together. Objectively. But stick with me for a second. Someone was good about telling her she was beautiful when she was a kid. So she believed it.

It became her truth. And so other people believe it too. I believed it for a little while. All the cheerleaders who follow her around believe it. No one even questions it."

"I did, secretly."

"Maybe you were jealous." He smiles.

"Whatever. But Rebecca Forman's 'truth' was just her perception."

"Right. But perception becomes truth if you can get people to see it your way. Truth is a much more fluid concept than you choose to believe it is."

"Do you know Zoe's truth? Have I even told you why she's running to the Grand Canyon?"

"No."

"She thinks she was abducted by aliens, and she thinks if she runs into the lightning, she can get back to them. That is her truth. Her reality. You can't tell me that if she can convince enough people, that will become true. Zoe can believe it till the cows come home, but there are no aliens traveling through lightning to take her back to their exoplanet."

"Till the cows come home?"

"It must be my new tattoo talking."

"How do you know? That there are no aliens?"

"There has to be something that we can know for sure. I know for sure that Zoe is disappointed in the way things are turning out. I know for sure that your friend Ethan did something to upset her. And that she didn't get into the schools she wanted to get into. She is stuck and embarrassed, so she created this story in her mind. She can't stand admitting that she might just be a regular schmo like the rest of us."

"Ethan is not my friend, number one, and none of us, you especially, is a regular schmo."

"The world seems to think we are regular schmos. Only regular schmos go to County College."

"So go somewhere else. You didn't even try, and now you're blaming the rest of the world for your schmohood."

I sigh, frustrated to tears at the prospect that he might be right. I never thought about how setting my sights so low was motivated by self-pity, and I don't like thinking about it in that way. "We have to rescue her before she hurts herself. Can we agree on that?" I manage to say.

The Peruvian man starts to play something soft and slow on the Incan flute, as if he were listening to us and wanted to help us transition from this crazy conversation back into the world where it's true that Danny loves me.

DEVOTION

That same crazy wind is howling when we get to the bus station in Flagstaff. The wind that was blowing during Ethan's party and before the tornado. A hot, steady wind that makes sinister, ghostly whistling noises when it sails through the cracks of the bus fuselage. Outside I see more tumbleweeds, rolling over themselves. Skeletal, dry, and spooky in the dark. Somehow we have to get from here to the canyon's rim before the storm hits. And where on the rim, I'm not exactly sure. It's large. Grand, in fact. How the hell am I supposed to find Zoe?

"How the hell are we supposed to find Zoe?" I say out loud.

"I thought you had a plan."

"Nope."

The bus station is not much bigger than the bus itself. It's in a little strip mall in the middle of an enormous flat basin surrounded by some tall scruffy mountains that are covered with patchy tufts of shrubs. They look like ugly slack necks in need of a shave. I can see them because of the full moon that hangs flat and silvery in the middle of the whole scene. It's eighty miles to the canyon, and it's eleven o'clock at night. We can't wait till morning, and all the shuttles have stopped.

"Taxi?" I suggest.

We find a phone book hanging from the one pay phone in the bus station, and we choose All Star Taxi. Our driver is prompt and gets to the bus station parking lot quickly.

"Can you take us to the Grand Canyon?" I ask him.

"It's closed," he says.

"How can the Grand Canyon be closed? Does someone zip it up for the night? Put a big pool cover over it or something? The Grand Canyon doesn't close, mister, and we need to get there now."

"Did you just call him *mister*?"

"For emphasis."

"That was cute."

"Only one road is open. To the South Rim."

"That's fine." That must mean Zoe is near the South Rim too, I think.

Before we slide into the backseat, I notice that our piping Peruvian friend is sitting on the steps. "Want a ride?" I ask him.

He shrugs and then gets up and throws his suitcase into the trunk. Danny and I are traveling light. All we have left is his wallet full of ice cream money and my big black sleeping-bag jacket that doesn't breathe and is now coated with a thin film of my sweat. Love does conquer all if Danny can love me while I'm wearing this thing.

Danny slides in first, I get in next to him, and the Peruvian man sits and closes the door. "In trouble?" he asks.

"A friend is. She's out there, and she's sort of losing her mind. She thinks that aliens are going to travel through this storm to visit her."

"Not is crazy," he says.

"Yes, is crazy," I say.

"Good friend no think friend is crazy. Machu Picchu? Easter Island? The pyramids? They have been here before. Left evidence. Maybe come again."

"Through the lightning?"

The man just shrugs and then takes a little nap, leaning his head against the window.

"Is crazy," I whisper to Danny. He smiles, and we try to fall asleep on top of each other. I can smell what's left of his worn-off deodorant, hear the little puffs of his breath. His fingertips dangle limply into the seat well, and I can't stop myself from touching the fleshy pads of his fingers and tracing the swirling prints. I love feeling the weight of his arm on top of me.

The cab climbs up and up and up to the village, where we drop off Alejandro, which we finally learn is what he is called. We watch him wander through the streets to the entrance of the campground. Then we continue on, and finally we reach the forest.

It's very woodsy around the rim, and dark except for the moon. There is a closed gate at the entrance to the park. Just a big metal pole swung horizontally across our path next to a booth where a ranger would normally collect our entrance fee. "This is as far as I can take you," the cabdriver says. "You better scoot quick before a ranger starts getting nosy."

We start to run then. The air is thin compared to what we're used to, and it smells like sage and piñon—a musky scent from the trees that smells faintly like something burning. When the path gets steep, we start to walk, until we finally make it to the Powell monument, the little turnout where buses pull over and visitors get their first good glimpse of the canyon.

When I see it in the distance, I start to sprint toward it. I can't wait to look over the edge. I walk past the plaque honoring this Powell guy who made maps—a long time ago, when it was difficult to make maps—and I stop at a flimsy post fence, the only thing between me and plummeting to my death. It's a miracle you don't hear reports of toddlers plummeting to their deaths every day in the Grand Canyon. *They really do nothing to prevent it,* I think.

And then I look.

It is huge. Even at night I can see the vastness of it. Your brain can't possibly take it all in, so your eyes do this thing where they make a poster out of it. They put it all into 2-D, so it looks like you're seeing a flat mural of the thing rather than the thing itself. A streetlamp and the moon provide enough light so that I can see the contrasting shadows of the layers upon layers of earth that have been worn away and chiseled into sharp earth art. It's the only place left on the planet where you cannot physically see a Starbucks in any direction for as far as you look.

Danny holds me around my waist, and we have a moment to breathe before the first clap of thunder sounds and echoes below us so that it feels like an earthquake. It's hard to recognize where the vibrations are coming from because the echo is so powerful.

"They're here," Danny jokes.

It's not funny, though. I run back to the parking lot so I can get a better vantage point of the canyon edges. I scan the perimeter for Zoe. For any traces of movement. "Zoe!" I yell. Danny joins me between the cracks of thunder, his deep voice booming and echoing across the forest.

Big forceful drops of rain start to pelt the dry earth and move tiny clouds of dirt around themselves. It's cold in the desert at night, and soon I am shivering—my calls to Zoe visible in clouds of icy white mist. Off to our left in the woods, I see a fire tower. A wooden structure built for the rangers to get a good look around. It's like an enormous lifeguard chair for the landlocked.

I climb it, the adrenaline lifting me higher and higher, until I can see above the trees. I see some leaves moving near Hopi Point. And then I find her crawling on her hands and knees through the brush.

"That way!" I yell to Danny, pointing to the south. "Hopi Point! And call 911!"

He gets a head start while I climb down the tower and then follow after him.

Danny is talking to her in a calm voice as I approach.

Except for her underpants and the beaded corn-pollen pouch around her neck, Zoe is naked. Her skin is splotched with dirt and scratched from the brambles, but she looks smooth and otherworldly. She is backing up toward the edge of the rock and looking toward the sky. A mile below, the Colorado River shoots directly toward us in a deep, dark, and jagged scar.

"Zoe!" I say, trying to catch my breath. "Where are your clothes?"

"I won't need them," she says, backing her feet closer to the edge and looking again toward the sky. It's just drizzling now, the rain creating a soft veil between us.

"Aren't you cold, Zo? Let's go down to the village and get some hot chocolate." I take a step toward her, and she holds up her hand. Her lips and the tint of her skin beneath the dirt are a pale slate blue.

"Don't come any closer." She reaches into the pouch and pulls something out of it.

"But Zoe."

"Stay there . . . Catch!" she says, and she throws me a small book that lands at my feet. I snatch it up before it gets too wet. It's a photo album. With a beaded cover that Zoe made herself. I don't have time to take a good look because I don't want to take my eyes off her. I think it is a photo catalog for my museum of intangible things. Audacity (Kermit), Gluttony (Squirrely, a man's triceps in my face, and me eating a mayonnaise sandwich), God (the tornado), Knowing what you want/Saying yes to life (Rosemarie), Destiny (me on the white buffalo), Betrayal (Old Faithful), Love (Danny and me at our slot machine), Luck (my tattooed hip).

"So you can remember when I'm gone. I think you can make it without me now. We didn't have a picture of the first one. What was it?"

"Insouciance," I say.

"Yeah. Insouciance. Stop giving a shit," she says. "You care too much." She inches even closer to the edge. A few pebbles start falling away and rolling down the face of the canyon.

"You don't have to go anywhere, Zoe. Come with us. It's time to go home. We need to see Noah."

"You have to take care of him for me, Hannah. You know what he needs, okay? You need to make sure he understands people." Her voice catches for a second. "People can be cruel. He needs to be able to read them." This is when she cries a little, a tear forging a track through the dirt on her face. "Take care of him, Hannah."

"Who's going to take care of me, Zoe? You can't just leave me with this," I say, holding up the photo album. "It's not enough."

"You have him," she says, pointing to Danny. "That's enough."

"No, Zoe, it's not enough," I say, and I think how my love for Danny, at the outer limits, might last until he goes to college. My love for Zoe is supposed to last through graduations and weddings and baby showers and games of bridge. Forever. "Come on, Zo," I say.

I take a step toward her. And she jumps.

"Zoe!" I scream, and I rush to the edge.

She's standing on a ledge five feet below.

"Just practicing," she says.

"Zoe. Really. This isn't funny." My heart is thudding in my chest.

A thin streak of lightning flashes on the other side of the canyon. *Where are the police?* I wonder. Danny called them.

"Come on, Zoe," Danny says. "Don't give up. We're going to go home and start over. Try harder. We can get out of that town. It's up to us to create our own lives."

"Exactly," Zoe says. "And mine is with them."

"Fine," I say.

"Fine what?" Zoe asks, getting a little shifty.

"If this is true, then let me come with you. Remember

that story I read to you by Astrid Lindgren? The one about the two brothers? And how they jumped off the cliff together rather than be left forever apart? I'll jump with you."

"It doesn't work that way."

"Why? If you won't come with me, then I will go with you," I say.

"That's courageous of you, Hannah, but I will go alone," she says.

A huge streak of lightning in the exact shape of the Colorado River crackles and lights up the sky behind us.

"Do we go now?" I ask her. I jump down to her ledge and grab her hand.

"Let go, Hannah," she says. "Stop bullshitting me."

Thunder claps and echoes, and an orange streak of lightning, again in the same tree-branch shape of the river, darts down and ignites the brush below us. Smoke from the tiny fire rises. I do not let go of her hand.

"Let go, Hannah," Zoe says again. Her eyes look at me desperately. Wildly. Sadly.

"No," I say.

I think of a terrorist attack or a natural disaster. One that happens in our town. One where we have to escape. Who would I rescue first? My mom? My Dad? Danny? For a second I try to fool myself into thinking it would be Danny. But it's not true. The first person I would look for is Zoe. I would find her first and dig her out from the rubble before I even thought of anyone else. I am bound to her in a way no one else would understand. "I'm going with you," I say calmly, boldly, resolutely.

She tries to squirm out of my grip. One last bolt of lightning, a more powerful one this time, sizzles past my ear as it slices through the sky directly at us. It's as if it were thrown at us by Thor. It makes a direct hit onto the ledge we are standing on. I feel it shock and reverberate through my feet. Electricity moves through my veins. I'm shocked just enough to let go of Zoe's hand for a second. But when I try to grab it back, she dives.

A perfect swan dive. Into the sky. I try to reach for her when another blinding bolt shoots into the rock, and I fall. I tumble through the brush, sliding down the side of the canyon, feeling hot pebbles and rocks lodging themselves deep beneath my skin. I tumble literally head over heels until somehow I grab onto a branch and stop my descent. I am huddled in the fetal position on a little ledge.

There is no sound left in my voice as I silently scream, "Zoe!" one more time into the canyon.

FORGIVENESS

They found nothing but the corn-pollen pouch. It was scorched and charred around the edges, some of the beads melted into flat colorful snail trails along the leather. Inside was a photo of Noah, his mouth twisted into an awkward sideways smile. On the back he had scribbled *joy* with a red crayon.

In a hospital somewhere near Flagstaff, doctors remove shards of ancient canyon rock from my torso and stitch up a gash in my thigh. I lie in the bed bandaged and sore, but with a beautiful view of the San Francisco Mountains that I can see through the slits of my half-open eyes.

It was not an accident. I really wanted to go with her. It was no elaborate ruse. When forced to make a choice, I chose her.

I look at sweet Danny sleeping next to me in a chair, and I remind myself that he doesn't need to know that. He could never understand. There are different versions of the truth.

He doesn't have to know all your secrets, I hear Zoe saying to me from wherever she ended up. *It's called discretion. See also: Mystery. Be mysterious, Hannah.*

Discretion, mystery, allure. Not my strong suits, I say back to her. Even though she is gone. Forever. And I have no idea what to do with my grief about that. I feel a leaden line of grief straight through my center: from my throat to my heart and down through my stomach. My body curls around it, protecting it. I can't imagine ever standing up straight again.

I look at Danny, his black wispy eyelashes interlaced against the daylight like a Venus flytrap. Our future is uncertain. This experience could either bond us or drive us apart. I don't know what I have left to give him in this moment. I can only fall into his arms.

I go to sleep in a painkiller-induced fog. They are trying to pump the life back into me with an IV filled with replacement tears. *I will just cry them out again*, I think. What's the use? I think that I hear my parents descending upon us. Their sharp footsteps in the hall. But it could be a dream. They don't say much, but in my dream I can see my mother's seething rage coming off her in gray waves. She will blame this on my father. As if he drove me across the country and pushed me off the edge.

He will dismiss her with a simple cruel glance. It's so easy for him to write her off.

They battle inside of me. His hatred for her. Her hatred

for him. It all adds up to some subtle hatred for me. I can't help but remind them of each other.

But they showed up, right? That's something. To take me home and help me start over. "Hi, Mom," I manage. She hugs me with her soft arms. And it feels good.

When I wake up again, Susan is here. She has Zoe's black hair, but it is thicker and rippled with streaks of long wavy grays. The rims of her eyes are red. The bags under them look black-and-blue.

"Hi," I mumble.

"I want to die," Susan says to me, holding her forehead in her hands.

"I know," I say back.

"Can you hear me right now, because there's something I need to say to you," she says.

I nod.

"This is not your fault."

"Okay," I whisper, and a tear squeezes out of the corner of my eye.

"I am her mother. And if there's one thing I know about Zoe, it's that there is no changing her mind once she has it made up." She breathes in, cries, and continues. "I would never blame you for this, okay, Hannah? I trust that you did your best."

"Okay," I say.

"If you couldn't help her, no one could."

My mother is standing in the doorway, leaning against the doorjamb, probably biting her tongue. I know somewhere in the back of her mind she is dying to ream into me. "What were you thinking?!" I can hear her say. "You think you're a psychologist now, hotshot?"

"I'm sorry," I say.

"It's not your fault," Susan says again.

It will be a long time before I can truly forgive myself, though, and stop having dreams about falling from the sky. And waking

up just before

I hit

the ground.

LIFE

We got off easy for "accomplice to Tasering and grand theft auto." I don't know how we got the judge to give us the same community service assignment, but she did, and now Danny and I have a built-in date, early Saturday mornings, where we prepare the day's meals for a women's homeless shelter. We have to wear hairnets.

On the menu today: fruit salad. We're learning to cut the meat of the grapefruit—the pink, pulpy part—from its membranes. It's called "supreming." We do a little "Stop in the Name of Love" choreography before we start. After we're finished, we meet in the walk-in and engage in some grapefruit-flavored kissing. Luckily the grapefruit smell drowns out the oniony sour milk–pickle odor that is a perpetual fixture inside the refrigerator.

"You are so hot in this," he jokes, tucking his rubber-gloved finger beneath the elastic of my hairnet and lifting it off.

I wrap one leg around his waist, and he grabs my athletic rear end, pulls me closer, and then cruelly breaks away, coming to his senses.

"Margaret wants her cottage cheese," he says.

"And you are the biggest tease."

He's sweet with the ladies, who drew a terrible lot in this life. When I see them, lining up for their coffee and cheese and cheap white-bread toast, I think, *There, but for the grace of God, go I.* Another thing I learned from AA.

On Sundays, I work with Ms. Brennan at Operation Save Our School. I share with her what I've learned from my attic days at the private school, and we try to figure out a way to fix Johnson High's curriculum. We're planning a walkout after Christmas, demanding to be educated.

Sunday evenings, I see my dad.

I'm helping him finally take the boat out of the water, on a balmy sixty-degree Christmas Eve in New Jersey, and I've decided to forgive him, because resentment can lead to health problems.

And it's Christmas. And Zoe's not here to fuel my anger and keep me strong and resistant to him. To stop me from being an enabler. "*How many chances does he get?*" I can hear her say from somewhere in outer space.

"So you lost the job for good, huh?" I ask him.

It's the cardinal rule of weathermanning. You cannot speak of global warming, ever. It's not reporting the weather

drunk that bothered the execs. Weatherpeople, like game-show hosts, are drunk all the time on the air. It's the only way they can survive their meaningless existence. But you cannot ever "acknowledge the existence of a large-scale climatological issue with its roots in the use of fossil fuels by humans." This is in every weatherman contract. It pisses off the advertisers. So I don't know how my father will find another job. He needs a Plan B.

"You're not supposed to acknowledge the existence of a large-scale . . ."

"I know, Hannah," he says.

"You can't go back to the weather center. The technology has surpassed you," I say to my father. We've hooked the boat to the trailer and have pulled it up the boat launch. We're waxing the bottom because that's what you're supposed to do before you put it in dry dock. We are doing a very cursory job, however. The boat is a piece of shit. "You don't even know how to use e-mail . . . Maybe you can come up with a schtick, like rapping the weather. I think I saw that on YouTube."

He continues squeaking the all-natural sea sponge along the scummy underside of the boat.

"Maybe you could take some computer classes. Or you could move to a very remote market. There are a lot of tornadoes in the Southeast these days." I scoop some more Turtle Wax from the container and spread it on the boat in a swirling circular motion. The sun is setting over the far side,

the Ethan Drysdale side, of the lake. It melts and drips like sweet butterscotch syrup over those who must have done something to deserve it. We observe from the shadows.

"Possibly. I have a contact in the traffic department at the local radio station. Traffic reports. On the sevens."

"You have a face for radio," I say.

"I guess I deserve that," he says. He continues to look down into his bucket. He can't look at me. His profile is still handsome. He has chiseled cheekbones and a strong masculine chin with a cleft in the middle. He actually has a face for television. "I plan to pay you back," he says.

"Whatever," I say. "Just stay sober. A day at a time. Work the program. I can take care of myself."

"Oh, you can, can you?" He finally looks at me.

"Well, I have to, don't I?"

"I guess I deserve that too," he says, looking back into his bucket.

As he wields the sponge, his hands still shake a little, which might be permanent at this point. There are only so many benders you can fully recover from. At least as a traffic reporter on the radio, he doesn't have to point to anything with a steady hand.

"What are you doing later?" he asks me. It breaks my heart, but I have to leave him alone on Christmas Eve.

"I have a thing," I tell him, and he just nods. "I can see you tomorrow, though. Is there a meeting?"

He brushes a tear away, sniffs, and nods. "Yeah. I'll go to a meeting. Watch a movie. I'll be okay."

"Okay," I tell him. "Hug?"

"Hug," he says, and he wraps me up in his familiar, warm arms.

"I miss her too, you know," he says as I'm walking away. "Who's going to keep me in line now? She was good at that. She saw right through me."

"You. You can keep yourself in line."

"Okay."

"Okay," I say as I walk to my car. "See you tomorrow."

"Okay," he says.

Noah planned the whole thing. He sent me an invitation in his chicken-scratch handwriting and told me to meet him in the woods. He also asked me to call Snozzberry, Zoe's favorite band, and have them meet us there too.

They're playing when I get there. Just an ambling instrumental number, perfect for accompanying people's processional down the path through the trees that Noah had outlined with flower petals.

My mom is here. And Susan. And Karen and Jen. Danny and I walk hand in hand, the soft pad of his finger tracing nervous circles inside my palm. No one knows what to expect.

A group of about thirty people arrive. Ms. Brennan. Ice. Even Rebecca. My father must have heard about it too, because although he may not have been invited, I notice his shadowy silhouette staring down at the scene from a nearby hilltop.

Julian comes up behind us and puts his soft arm around my shoulder. He's wearing a rabbit-fur jacket.

"Where did you find that?" I ask him, pointing to the fur coat.

"A friend gave it to me. And don't ask me who my friend is, because if I reveal that information, I'll be forced to drink gasoline," he jokes. The brown rabbit fur flanks either side of his chest, but he has the zipper open to his belly button, revealing his smooth hairless pectoral muscles. He has brown eyes and a willowy body. His sandy blond hair looks perfect, as if he'd just come from a photo shoot with *Teen Beat.*

"You need different friends," I tell him.

"That's what college is for, sweetheart. You should try it. Come with me," he begs, holding out his hand. "You can live in my dorm room and be my pet." Somehow, he got into Columbia. Soon he'll be lost in the city, becoming fabulous and better off. But I can tell he is terrified.

"You can't have a fag hag for a pet, sweetheart." I brush my fingers down his cheek.

"Oooo. Hannah. You said *fag.*"

"I did. But it was in a certain context."

"That's what I love about you. You're so contextual." He twirls me in toward him and kisses me on top of my head.

"That doesn't even make sense," I say.

"Hannah. It's starting," Danny says, and I join him at the edge of the "installation." In a clearing around our weeping willow, Noah has arranged all of his favorite pieces from Zoe's exhibits. The beating heart impaled with the kitchen knife, the flowered couch, the marionette peacock, the bill of rights written on the roll of toilet paper. He even, somehow, mysteriously, has dredged up my rusted hot dog cart from the lake and decorated it with dozens of red roses. In the trees he has hung all of Zoe's designs. They glisten and wave in the wind like flags of fabulosity. In the center, on the ground, Noah has arranged the torn-out pages of Zoe's copy of *On the Road* into four enormous letters, spelling out the word LIFE.

I had forgotten until this moment that "Zoe" actually means life in Greek.

He cues the band to play Zoe's favorite song, and when they are done, he lights a fuse. The letters, one by one, spark and sizzle alight. And they burn brightly with a blue and orange fire. When they're done, a couple of bottle rockets shoot off over the lake, illuminating the willow and the grove and all the crying people around it. "Thank you," he says robotically. "I know she can see this, where she is."

His mom scoops him into a flying hug. And the band

keeps playing as we mill around a little, drinking eggnog and apple cider. I can't stay for long, though. No one can understand exactly what grief feels like for another person, because depending on your relationship to the deceased, you feel your grief differently from everyone else on the planet. I won't say my grief was deeper. But I will say I can't stay for long. It feels like my heart has been scooped out with a melon baller.

"Tomorrow will be better," I promise Danny through my tears. "But now I need to go." He's been pretty understanding about my good days and my bad days. More understanding than he needs to be. "We'll try again tomorrow?"

"Yes," he says. "Merry Christmas, Hannah."

"Merry Christmas."

My mom drives me home, and we lay together head to foot like a pair of shoes in a shoebox on the couch listening to really old Patti Page Christmas carols. People's Christmas lights blink on and off in the reflection of the lake outside our window. There is no snow. She holds me as I promise to shed my last tear about this, and she tells me things will get better.

And I believe her. Because in some ways they already have.

HAPPINESS
(EVER AFTER)

The rest of my life has been spent repairing the Zoe-shaped hole she left in my heart. And since she gave me a recipe for doing that, I've been quite successful at it. I define what I want and have the audacity to go after it. And whenever possible, to the appropriate questions, I say yes. Do you want to eat oysters? Do you want to scuba dive? Do you want to photograph zebras in Kenya? Do you want to finally visit Sweden? Want to go for a run? Meditate? Go skiing? Save the polar bears? Will you marry me? Yes.

I let myself be gluttonous sometimes.

And I'm never rude, necessarily, but there are times when I remind myself to stop giving a shit.

I have a framed picture of me and Danny in our crimson and white graduation gowns, tucked away in a box in my closet. His eyes are bright and gleaming, and they are crinkled delightfully in the corners. His knuckly fingers clasp tightly around my shoulder. He was my first love. And even now, when I look at it, there's a happy-sick twinge in my heart.

But they call it first love for a reason.

Because other loves come after that. Especially in lives as long as ours.

I have left behind what tethered me to the lake. The sadness. The self-pity. The dark tentacles of the murky sea monster only I could see. And I have come to appreciate the ocean. How the sun and salt together can leave things weightless, easy, and smooth around the edges. Like sea glass and driftwood.

I write a letter once a month to Noah, about thrift or tenacity or denial or honesty or hypocrisy or beauty, and I send it to him at his office in NASA, where he studies a very specific exoplanet around an M-dwarf star between the constellations of Cygnus and Lyra . . . and he searches for life.